# DANNY ORLIS
## AND THE
# BID FOR VICTORY

# DANNY ORLIS
## AND THE
# BID FOR VICTORY

BERNARD PALMER

*Danny Orlis and the Bid for Victory*
© 2024 by Bernard Palmer
All rights reserved. First edition 1969.
Second edition 2024.



*Cover image: Adobe Firefly*
*Character illustrations: John Ball*
*Editor: Charlene Miskimen*

Aneko Press *Youth*

www.anekopress.com

Aneko Press, Life Sentence Publishing, and our logos are trademarks of Life Sentence Publishing, Inc.
203 E. Birch Street
P.O. Box 652
Abbotsford, WI 54405

**JUVENILE FICTION / Religious / Christian / Action & Adventure**

Paperback ISBN: 979-8-88936-050-6

eBook ISBN: 979-8-88936-051-3

10  9  8  7  6  5  4  3  2  1

Available where books are sold

# CONTENTS

# CHAPTER 1

# THE HANG-UP

Sunday morning broke cold and raw. The wind growled through the naked trees and clogged the rivulets from melting snow with wafer-thin coats of ice. It would not be long until the lawns would begin to wear a gossamer-green tint, like a halo that signaled the arrival of spring and warm growing days to come. Now, however, that day seemed distant and far away, the sort of thing one dreamed about but never expected to see.

Lester and Vivian McCloud noted none of those things as they got up and dressed. The bleak, sunless morning only reflected the ice that had lain unmelting within their very beings. Their son Fritz was dead. Nothing could change that fact. Now the funeral was over, all the relatives had gone home, and they were faced with the problem of living. It didn't seem worth the effort. Mechanically they dressed for

Sunday school and church. They hadn't talked about going. They just assumed they would.

Connie, however, was still in bed at nine o'clock.

"Did you say anything about asking her to go with us this morning, Vi?" Lester asked.

His wife nodded. The lines on her tired face told the story of the shock and sorrow that had overtaken the family.

"I had quite a long visit with her yesterday, Lester. She said that she had decided she wasn't going to church anymore."

"I still think we ought to talk to her. She can't wall herself off from people. Life has to go on."

Connie's mother went to her bedroom and knocked on the door.

"Connie."

No answer.

"Connie! May I come in?" She had to repeat the question two or three times before there was any indication that she had been heard.

"I guess so," the girl mumbled, her voice guarded.

Mrs. McCloud paused, her hand on the doorknob and her head lowered, as though in prayer. Then she went inside and closed the door behind her. Connie was sitting up in bed, a petulant sneer pulling the corner of her mouth downward.

"What do you want, Mom?" she asked, with obvious irritation.

Vivian McCloud sat down casually on the edge of

the bed as she used to do so often when her daughter was a little girl.

"Dad and I would like to have you go with us to Sunday school and church this morning," she said.

Anger blazed in the girl's eyes and her lips curled.

"Church!" she exploded. "How many times do I have to tell you that I'm not going to church and Sunday school anymore?"

Mrs. McCloud was not shocked. Only very deeply hurt and concerned.

"I'm sorry for you, Connie," she said quietly. "I'm very sorry for you."

That was more than Connie could stand. She could take her mother's anger and the hurt in her face. But pity was something else. Suddenly she was furious.

"You don't have to feel sorry for me," she retorted curtly. "I've finally come to the place where I see exactly how useless going to church really is." Her voice was bitter. "Going to church has never done anything for anybody!"

"Connie," Mrs. McCloud said, "you shouldn't talk that way."

The girl swung her feet over the side of the bed.

"I don't see why not," she replied. "Church has never done anything for me or for anyone I know. It's just a farce!"

"Fritz didn't believe that way. You know what a tremendous testimony he had."

"That's just it!" Once she had begun to speak all

the pent-up doubt and bitterness gushed out in a torrent of words like water released by a bursting dam. "Fritz believed everything he was told about being a Christian, and he really lived his faith. He did more for the Lord in a week than most believers do in a year – and what happened?"

Mrs. McCloud nodded. "God's ways are not our ways," she said quietly.

"I've heard all of those fancy platitudes I want to hear!" Connie got to her feet and stared down at her mother. "How can God be a God of love and let someone like Fritz be killed? If there really is a God who cares for us, why didn't He let Johnny Larson get killed and let Fritz live? Johnny was the one who was living in sin and mocking God and all that He stands for."

Vivian responded with gentleness to her daughter's outburst. "Maybe that's the reason it happened the way it did, Connie."

The girl's eyes narrowed. "What do you mean?"

"We can't understand why God does what He does, Connie, and we probably shouldn't try. But this might be one reason things happened as they did. God *is* a God of love. Fritz was a fine Christian, and there's no question that he's in heaven now. But Johnny didn't know Christ as his Savior. If he had been killed, he would have gone to hell." She took a deep breath. "Perhaps God spared Johnny to give him another chance to make his decision for Christ."

That seemed to stop Connie. The hurt in her eyes deepened. "I don't see how you can even talk that way, Mom," she said. "If I didn't know you better, I'd almost think you didn't love Fritz."

Vivian McCloud tried to explain to Connie how she and her husband felt about Fritz's death; how it was clear to them that it was the will of the Lord, and that they had to accept it as such. But it was as though the girl wasn't listening. She sat down again beside her mother on the edge of the bed, her eyes wide and staring. She acted like a robot who moved mechanically but was devoid of feeling.

Several times her mother asked her questions, but Connie gave no indication that she heard them, let alone answered. At last Mrs. McCloud reluctantly gave up and went back to the living room.

"Well, did you accomplish anything?"

She shook her head. "I can't do anything with her, Lester," she said. "She sits there as though she doesn't even know that I'm talking to her."

Mr. McCloud tugged at the lobe of his ear. "That's what I was afraid of. When I've tried to talk with her, I've felt the same way."

Vivian sat down across from her husband.

"Maybe we ought to talk with Pastor Reeves about her. She's always had a great deal of respect for him. Perhaps he could help her."

* * *

It was two weeks after Fritz's death before Connie could bring herself to go back to work. Even then it was more difficult than she had thought it would be. She felt the strain that morning as she and Winifred Blair drove down to the office together.

"Feel all right?" Winnie asked her.

"I guess so." There was no life in her voice.

"You don't have to go to work this morning if you don't want to," her friend told her. "You know what the manager said. You don't have to come back to work until you feel like it. You'll still have a job, regardless."

"I know, but Dad and Mom are getting on me all the time. I'd rather come to work than to have to listen to them hounding me about moping around all day."

They left the car and started into the building. It wasn't going to be easy to work that morning, even with Winnie beside her. Everybody would be so kind and considerate, so concerned about her welfare that she wouldn't be able to stand it. It would be a great deal easier, she told herself doggedly, if they'd all act as though nothing had happened. Then she might be able to forget, at least for a little while.

At the door she stopped and turned to her best friend.

"I–I don't know whether I can go in or not," she murmured.

"What's the matter?"

"If I see Ted Larson, I–I'll just die."

Winifred glanced in both directions as though Ted might be coming to work at that very moment, but when she spoke, she talked as though there was no chance that Connie would meet him.

"He's probably out on service calls by this time. They've been terribly busy lately."

"Maybe." Doubt crept into Connie's voice. "And maybe not. But even if I don't see him this morning, he'll be in sometime today. He always is. And I can't stand to see him. Not ever!"

"But, Connie, you can't blame him for what happened to your brother. It wasn't his fault."

"Maybe not." Connie stared at her friend as though she felt betrayed. "But I'm not going to see him anymore. I'm never going to talk to him again! And if you see him, you can tell him that for me."

"But, Connie!"

"After what his brother did to my family, I can't help it! I'm not going to speak to him again!"

Winnie said no more. It was useless to try to talk with her friend when she was that way. She wouldn't listen to anything anyone said. All she could do for Connie was to pray for her.

Connie walked mechanically to the office and took her place. The day was a busy one and she scarcely had time to think about anything until the morning coffee break. She didn't plan on going into the lunchroom at all that day. She was going to stay on the job during the coffee break periods and go to the cafe around the corner for lunch so she would be sure she wouldn't have Ted Larson come up and try to talk with her again.

She really didn't know how he could bring himself to see her after what his brother had done to her family. And to make matters worse, the judge hadn't even kept Johnny locked up. He was out on bail. That showed what Ted and his parents thought of the whole affair. And what the authorities thought of it too. It was just an escapade – a little trouble that Johnny's dad would be able to get him out of. At least they were going to try. But they'd soon find out that everything wasn't going their way.

The whole town liked Fritz and few people could stand Johnny. The judge would find out that the opinion of the people in town would be against him if he was easy on Johnny.

That was one good thing. He ought to have to pay for what he'd done. And he was going to if there was anything she could do about it.

Suddenly Connie remembered that her own father had actually led Johnny to the Lord. She didn't see how he could even have talked to him. At the very thought of the boy who had been driving the car that hit and killed Fritz, a revulsion welled up within her. She didn't know how her dad could have forced himself to talk to Johnny.

There was something else that concerned her almost as much. She couldn't help but wonder if this had just been a way Johnny had used to get on the good side of her parents. He felt bad about what he had done. There was no doubt about that. But he probably thought things would go easier for him if he told them that he wanted to become a Christian.

And her dad would fall for it too. He was so naive he would believe anything he was told. But not her. She wasn't being taken in. She didn't know just what she could do, but she was going to see that Johnny Larson paid for killing Fritz if it was the last thing she ever did. She would see that the law punished him. She didn't know how long he could be jailed for what he had done, but however long it was, it wasn't half long enough.

The very thought of Johnny set her whole being trembling with hatred. She was still thinking about him when Winnie stopped and asked her to go to the lunchroom with her.

Connie shook her head. "No, thanks," she said. "I'm not taking a coffee break this morning."

"But I don't want to sit by myself," Winnie told her. "Come on in and sit with me."

"There'll be other people in there. You won't be alone."

"But I don't want anybody else. I want you, Connie."

Connie hesitated, leaning forward so no one else could hear her. "You haven't seen Ted go into the lunchroom, have you?" she asked.

Winnie shook her head. "I haven't seen him all morning."

Connie went reluctantly into the lunchroom with her friend. Ted wasn't there, but a short time later he came in. His handsome face was solemn and lined with grief, and his eyes were red-veined. He looked at her and then quickly looked away, his face flushing. She was afraid that he was going to come over, but he sat at a table as far from her as possible. He gulped his coffee and bolted for the door as soon as he finished.

It was some time before Connie could speak. "I thought you said he wouldn't be here." Her voice was harsh and accusing.

"I didn't think he would be," her friend answered. "But he didn't embarrass you by being friendly, did he?"

Connie had to admit that he had not. "He was the one who was embarrassed, and he should have been. If I had a brother like his, I don't think I'd ever be able to hold my head up again!"

The others in the lunchroom could not help overhearing and turned to stare at them.

Winnie laid a hand tenderly on Connie's arm. "People are listening." She scarcely mouthed the words.

"I don't care. If they don't know how I feel about Johnny Larson and what he did to Fritz, I want them to know. I'm not ashamed of it."

She broke down suddenly, tears coursing down her cheeks. She got to her feet, scraping the chair back noisily, and fled from the room.

# CHAPTER 2

# HARVEY'S STORY

Connie refused to go out that night, even with Winnie.

"I just can't go tonight," she said. "If I do, everyone will turn and stare at me."

"That's your imagination."

"No, it's not. I've had it happen a lot of times." She picked up a magazine and thumbed the pages nervously. "You don't know what it's like. If I go anywhere, I'm certain to hear somebody whisper, 'There's that McCloud girl. Her brother was killed in a car accident by the drunk.' I'd rather not go anywhere than to have to listen to them."

Winnie said nothing.

"And that's not the worst. It never fails that someone comes up to me and makes such a big show of being sympathetic. When it happens, I feel like telling them to be quiet and leave me alone."

"If you won't go with me to the youth meeting tonight, would it be all right if I come over and see you?"

Connie's smile flashed warmly. "Oh, I'd love that."

* * *

Winnie went to the McCloud home a few minutes after seven, and she and Connie were sitting alone in the living room. Winnie had been trying for some time to switch the subject to spiritual things but without success. Now she took a deep breath and plunged in.

"I missed you at church again Sunday."

The muscles in Connie's face hardened and her blue eyes flashed. "I've already told you how I feel about church, Winnie. I'm through with it. Remember?"

There was a brief silence.

"I can understand how you feel, Connie," her friend said, "but that won't solve anything for you. It will only make your problems worse."

"That's a matter of opinion," she snapped.

"You need the church," Winnie continued, "and the church needs you. You can't wall yourself off this way. It isn't right."

Connie tossed her head impatiently.

"Maybe I used to need the church," she retorted. "But if I did, I'm past that part of my life. Anyway, if God could let Fritz be killed, He's not too interested in us. As far as I'm concerned, I'm through with the church."

Winnie sat there feeling uneasy. The fact that God had allowed Fritz to be killed didn't mean He didn't love people. Winnie knew that, but how could she explain God's ways to her friend? How could she make her understand?

Connie's lower lip quivered, and she gave every indication of being about to cry when there was a knock at the door. The girls sat up suddenly.

"Are you expecting company?" Winnie asked.

Connie shook her head.

The knock sounded once more.

"You answer it, Winnie. I don't feel like talking to anyone right now."

She got to her feet and would have fled, but she was not in time. Winifred opened the door to reveal a tall, handsome blond man two or three years older than herself.

Winnie greeted him.

He seemed surprised at seeing her at the door, taken slightly aback because it wasn't answered by someone he knew and recognized.

"Is this the McCloud residence?"

Before Winifred could reply, Connie came back to the center of the room. "Yes," she said. "Do you want to see my father?"

He stepped inside uncertainly, and she recognized him as one of the new teachers at the high school.

"I–I guess your dad is the one member of the family that I've met," he said. "But to tell you the truth, I don't know for sure who I want to talk to. I–I mean–I suppose I ought to talk to him." He was obviously embarrassed. "My name's Harvey Rush."

Connie introduced herself and Winnie.

"Won't you sit down?" she asked, suddenly remembering her manners. "Dad will be back in a little while."

"Maybe I will." He took a chair near the door and for a time squirmed nervously. A fleeting minute later he continued. "I–I've just come from talking with Pastor Reeves."

A strange look gleamed in Connie's eyes. His statement had surprised her. The new teacher didn't exactly look the type to be religious.

"You–you have?" she echoed.

He nodded seriously.

"I–I helped coach the backfield when I came to Fairview last fall, so I–I got to know your brother quite well. I worked closely with him."

"Oh." Connie's voice was thin and far away.

"Fritz was different than the other kids I've come in contact with when I've been coaching," he said, breathing heavily. "When he talked to me about that–that religion of his, he really got to me, only I couldn't let him know it."

The teacher's voice broke, and it was a full minute before he could speak again. When he could go on, however, he spoke hesitantly and with such great emotion that he stirred both Connie and her friend.

"After he was killed," the teacher said, "and I heard that sermon the minister brought at the funeral, I couldn't sleep – or even think of anything else except the God that Fritz was always talking about. Then, today something happened that–"

Connie got nervously to her feet. Talk like this was disturbing. It bothered her, but she didn't know why.

"I think you'd better wait and talk to Dad," she said. "He should be home any time now."

But Harvey Rush was so worked up he didn't even hear her.

"Today I finally decided that I've been fooling around with this thing long enough. I went over to the minister's house, and he introduced me to Christ." A huge smile split his face. "I–I gave my heart to Christ!"

Winnie broke in quickly. "How wonderful!"

"I just had to tell somebody, so I came over here," he continued. "I figured you and your parents would like to know what Fritz did for me by talking to me."

Connie's eyes narrowed and her lithe body stiffened. This was the sort of talk that Pastor Reeves, Danny and Kay Orlis, her parents, and Jim Morgan used. It was the sort of talk she was trying to turn her back on. She hadn't expected to hear it from someone like the schoolteacher who sat before them. Connie's face went ashen, and her lips trembled slightly.

"If you'll excuse me, I–I have a terrible headache."

* * *

Basketball practice at the grade schools in Fairview started early and lasted well into the spring. The three schools in town played a round robin schedule; the winner then competed in games with schools from out of town. Doug and Del Davis both went out for the team, but as it turned out, at the start of the season, they had other problems than basketball.

Their grades were not too good, and the principal called Danny in to talk with him about it. After that, the situation changed. Doug and Del worked harder at their lessons than they had ever worked since coming to Fairview to live with Danny and Kay. Their grades soon reflected the added effort. Danny congratulated them on it.

"You boys are both doing good work in school now," he said. "I want you to know that I'm proud of you."

Doug grinned. "Believe you me, I'm not going to let my grades get in such bad shape again. It's a lot easier to keep the grades up than it is to get them up after they're down."

"That's true with school or work or anything else," Danny told them. "If you've learned that lesson, this experience has been worth a great deal to you."

Soon Doug spoke again, offhandedly, as though it didn't really matter. But Danny could tell that whatever was on his mind did matter a great deal to him.

"Are you going to be flying anywhere tomorrow, Danny?" he asked.

"I don't think so, why?"

"I thought maybe you'd like to come over and watch our basketball team play Riverton's grade school team tomorrow night."

"That sounds as though it ought to be okay." Danny glanced at Del. "Are you going to be playing too?"

Del colored.

"Well–" he began hesitantly.

Doug spoke up. "We'll both be suited up."

By this time Del's cheeks flamed. He was staring down at his plate.

"I'll be suited up, all right." The words lashed out bitterly. He pivoted to face his brother. "You'll start the game the way you did in practice today, but I won't. I won't even get off the bench."

Danny's voice was calm. "Don't let it shake you, Del," he said. "God doesn't give all of us the same abilities. What if Doug does play basketball better than you do? There are other things that you do better than Doug."

The hurt was deep in the boy's young eyes. "Like what?"

With that he pushed back noisily from the table and stormed into the bedroom he shared with his brother. Kay looked after him tenderly.

"Do you think I ought to go in and talk to him, Danny?" she asked.

He shook his head. "Not right now. I think he'd rather be alone."

After dinner that evening Danny and Doug went into the living room and sat down.

"What's the scoop on Del?" Danny spoke softly. "Isn't he any good as a basketball player?"

"He's not as bad as he thinks he is. The trouble is that he can't shoot."

Danny nodded understandingly. "I knew a guy like that when I was in high school," he said. "He could handle the ball all right, and he was fast enough to have made almost any high school team, but he didn't have an eye for the basket."

The silence hung between them.

"If Del doesn't make the team," Doug said at last, "I don't think I'll play basketball anymore either."

Danny stared at him. "I don't believe I follow you."

"I just said that I'm not going keep playing basketball if Del doesn't get to play. We've always done things together, and we're not going to stop now."

Danny did not answer him immediately, but when he did, his voice was gentle and understanding. "Do you think that will help Del?" he asked.

"I don't know whether it will help him or not, but that doesn't make any difference. We stick together."

"I can understand exactly how you feel, Doug. And I've got to admire you for it. But let's stop and think seriously about this for a minute. If you don't stay out for basketball, is that going to help Del to play any better than he does now?"

The boy looked up at Danny and then away quickly.

"I suppose not."

"If things were turned around, would you want Del to quit playing just because you weren't able to make the team?"

There was no answer.

"You boys look so much alike that most people can hardly tell you apart, but you're still individuals. And God didn't necessarily give you the same traits and abilities. He expects you to use the talent He gave you, and He expects Del to use the talent He gave to him."

Doug swallowed hard. "I sure wish Del had made the team," he said lamely. "I don't even want to play without him."

"You go out and play anyway, Doug. That's best for both you and Del."

* * *

Danny and Kay went to the junior high school gymnasium for the game with Riverton. Both Doug and Del were in uniform, but it was obvious that only Doug would be in the starting lineup. Del was standing listlessly in one corner of the floor, a few feet away from the rest of the squad.

Danny shook his head. "Del sure doesn't act as though he expects to get in the game today," he said.

"If the coach would only let him play a minute or two, I don't think he would feel quite so bad."

Doug started the game at forward position. He was shorter than the guys on either team but made up for his lack of height with speed. He took the tip from center at the opening whistle, dribbled along the sideline, faked past the Riverton man guarding him, and fired a quick pass to the Fairview center who was moving up fast. He missed the basket, but Tim Porter, the other forward, got the rebound and dumped the ball in to open the scoring. A shout went up from the crowd.

Danny turned to Kay. "Doug's a nifty ball handler," he said. "If he gets a little height to him in the next few years, Fairview's really going to be able to use him. He ought to make a top-notch basketball player."

Kay was scarcely listening. "I wish the coach would put Del in for a minute or two," she said, "just so he could feel that he'd had a part in the game."

"He might," Danny said," but only if Fairview can pile up enough of a lead."

But the Fairview quintet was not able to get a commanding lead. They inched ahead in the first quarter, only to lose their gain in the opening minutes of the second half. It was not until the waning moments of the final stanza that the hometown five were able to get in front again. And when the game was finally over, they had won by a scant three points.

Later that night, at home, DeeDee was still flushed with excitement.

"I yelled so loud I can hardly talk," she said.

Doug shrugged his shoulders.

"You aren't telling us anything we didn't know," he said, scoffing. "We could hear you all over the gym!"

Del broke in quickly.

"Yeah, everybody on the bench was wondering who that crazy girl was who was yelling so loud." He grimaced. "I was sure glad they didn't know that you were my sister. I'd never have been able to live it down."

She made a face at him. "I wasn't yelling for either one of you," she retorted. "So there."

"You didn't have to tell us that either," Doug said. "We know who you were yelling for."

Scarlet stained twin dots in either cheek. It was a moment before she could answer.

"I was yelling for the whole team."

"You can't kid us. You were yelling your head off for Tim Porter. Every time he'd get the ball, we'd hear you yell, 'Go, Tim! Go!'"

"Yeah, and it sure messed him up. Every time you yelled at him, he got so shook up he double dribbled or fell down or let Riverton steal the ball. You could've cost us the whole game, or didn't you know that?"

"Doug Davis!" DeeDee cried, the words choking

in her throat. "That's not true! Why–" She sputtered helplessly.

"I was never so embarrassed in my whole life," Del put in.

"Just you wait!" she warned darkly. Then she turned to Kay. "It's not true, Kay. They're just making all of that up so they can tease me. I wasn't yelling for Tim Porter."

"It wouldn't have hurt anything if you had been yelling for him," Kay said. "Lots of people yell for different players during a game."

"But not for the same reason DeeDee was yelling," Doug continued. "She's crazy about him. That's why."

By this time both boys were grinning impishly. Kay looked at them and then back at their sister.

"We were at the game, DeeDee," she said, smiling. "And you didn't embarrass us by your yelling. In fact, we didn't even notice it."

She eyed her brothers triumphantly.

"So there!"

The conversation at dinner was about the basketball game. Del said little. When their family devotions were over and the kids were about ready for bed, Danny went into the boys' room. They were just finishing their English.

"Del," Danny said, "I've been doing some thinking about your basketball playing."

A frown marred the boy's handsome young face.

"What've you been thinking?" he wanted to know.

"That I must be awful lousy or I'd have gotten in the game this afternoon?"

"Not at all." Danny pulled up a chair and sat down. "Doug tells me that you handle the ball pretty well."

"That's right," Doug broke in. "He does."

"You're the only guy who thinks so."

"No, Del," his brother countered, "the coach told me that your biggest trouble is shooting baskets. He said that if you had a better shooting eye, you'd have it made."

Del was not so easily consoled. "That's a big 'if.'"

Danny leaned forward, playing absentmindedly with the pen he had picked up.

"I wouldn't say that. Some guys can shoot baskets naturally; others have to learn how. That's what I had to do."

Del brightened noticeably. "You did?" he repeated.

"I sure did," Danny told him. "You see, I was raised on the Angle where I couldn't do much practicing with a basketball. And when I got into high school, I could handle the ball all right, but I didn't know how to shoot."

Del's interest increased. "What'd you do about it?"

"Dad put up a goal for me that summer, and I spent a couple of hours a day practicing."

Slowly the lights died in Del's eyes. And with it, some of the life that had sprung up.

"You mean you had to wait until summer before you could do anything about it?"

"I had to wait until the snow melted and it got warm enough so I could be outside and handle a basketball."

The boy sighed wearily. "That's not going to help," he moaned. "It won't do a thing for me this year."

Danny got to his feet. "Well, I'll see you guys in the morning."

Del followed him to the door. "Thanks, Danny."

"Sure." Danny patted him affectionately on the shoulder. "Everything's going to work out."

# CHAPTER 3

# RELEASE FOR CONNIE

**D**oug continued to play on the school basketball team. He was high-point man for two games in a row and one of the most effective players on defense. He consistently held his man on the opposing team to the lowest scoring.

Del was finally able to get into a game. It was near the end of the third quarter and Fairview was well in the lead, but by the time the coach put him in, he was so tense that he made a miserable flop of things. He fouled twice in as many minutes, and threw a long pass away. It was only a minute or two until he was back on the bench again, his face flushed with embarrassment.

Danny and Kay hadn't been able to go to the game, and when the triplets came home, they did not mention that Del had gotten to play or that Fairview had won again. At last Danny turned to Doug.

"Well, how'd the game turn out?"

"Okay." His voice was thin and expressionless.

"Did we win?"

"Sure." His tone indicated that he didn't particularly care whether they had won or not. "We knocked 'em off 32 to 19."

"You don't sound very happy about it."

"It was a good game, I guess." Doug pushed his chair back from the table.

For the first time since they began to talk about basketball that evening, Danny glanced at Del. The boy's face was white and drawn, and he did not lift his gaze from his plate. Danny changed the subject quickly.

"Well, I've got something besides basketball on my mind tonight," he said. "How'd you guys like to go rabbit hunting one of these Saturdays?"

Their faces lit up expectantly.

"Sounds great," Del exclaimed.

"Hank Blair has some new property northwest of here that he wants to look over on the first nice Saturday. He says there are a lot of rabbits around there and suggested that we bring our guns and go along if we'd like to hunt."

"Are you going to let us hunt, Danny?" Del asked.

Danny nodded. "Hank said he'd help one of you, and I can help the other."

Del bristled. "We don't need anyone to help us. We already know how to handle guns."

Danny nodded. "I know you had a little experience when you were in Guatemala," he said, "but a little more instruction won't hurt any. It's so important for a person to know how to handle a gun safely."

"But–"

"I started hunting with my dad when I was about your age," Danny continued as though he had not even heard Del's protest. "But he kept working with me until I was fifteen before he felt that I knew enough about gun safety to go out alone."

That seemed to satisfy Del. The frown left his face, and he asked Danny several questions about the place where they would be hunting.

"I can't tell you much about it," Danny continued, "because I've never been there myself. But Hank says it's mostly second-growth timber. I understand it borders a lake, and there's a little cleared land and some swamp. From the way he described it, it ought to be good rabbit country."

* * *

Connie tried to keep from thinking about Johnny Larson and the trial that was coming up in a few days, but she could not put her thoughts aside. Every morning, every night, brought Johnny's trial closer and closer. Her own tension continued to grow.

She was going to the trial to see what happened, she reasoned. She was going there to watch him squirm – to see him suffer the way he had made her and her parents suffer. It would give him a little taste of what he had put them through.

At the dinner table one evening a few days before the hearing, she informed her dad and mom of what she was going to do. She saw the disapproval on their faces, and it infuriated her.

"Don't try to talk me out of it," she informed them. "I've made up my mind. I don't care what anybody says. I'm going to be at that trial."

Her father leaned forward.

"I know how you feel, my dear, but do you think it's wise? It will just make things harder for you."

She stared at him incredulously. "Harder?" Her voice rose. "It won't be harder for me, Dad. It's going to be easier after I've seen him punished. He'll be an example to anyone else who might have an idea he can go out on the highway when he has been drinking and get away with it. It might stop some of the drinking the kids in high school are doing."

"'Vengeance is mine. I will repay, says the Lord,'" Mr. McCloud told her quietly. "Connie–"

She focused on him, eyes narrowing.

"You can talk like that!" she exploded. "I'm going to see Johnny Larson punished for killing Fritz! I'm going to see him get what he deserves."

Lester McCloud took a long breath and expelled the air in a thin stream. It hurt him to see his daughter that way, to see anger and hatred distorting her pretty face into something almost ugly. It hurt to hear her voice take on a harsh, strident quality that was so foreign to her. And there was so little he could do to help.

"Connie! Connie!" There was tenderness and pity in his words. "You can only hurt yourself with hate like that."

"Hurt myself?" she echoed. "I've already been hurt more than I can ever be hurt again!" Tears trembled in her voice.

Her dad picked up a fork and toyed with it, not even realizing that he had anything in his hand.

"There's been a real change in Johnny since he accepted Christ as his Savior."

The girl pushed back from the table and stood. This was something else she could not understand. She knew that Johnny's soul was as precious in the sight of the Lord as that of Fritz and anyone else. But how could her dad go and talk with him after what he had done to Fritz? She could not understand it.

The following day Ted Larson came into the lunchroom while she was there and stood uneasily near the door. Connie looked up. Their eyes met and held fixedly, as though under the control of some force greater than either of them. After a while she flushed crimson.

Ted shifted uncertainly from one foot to the other. It was obvious that he wanted to turn on his heel and leave, but he could not. With wooden movements he came over to the table where she was sitting.

"Connie?" he said softly.

She would not speak to him.

"Connie," he repeated. "I'd like to talk to you. May I–I sit down?"

"I don't care." Her lips curled about the words, and she shot them out bitterly. "I was about to leave anyhow."

He sat down across from her.

"Don't go yet, Connie," he repeated. "I've been wanting to talk to you for so long."

She did not reply, but neither did she leave. She sat there, still flushed, staring down at her coffee.

"You'll never know how–how miserable I've been since–since that accident," he began, moistening his lips uneasily. "I'd gladly change places with Fritz if I could. I want you to know that."

There was an anguish and desperation in his voice that she had never heard before – an anguish that bit into the very depths of her soul. She started to reply hotly, but stopped. How could she be so cruel to one who already felt so terrible?

"It hasn't been easy for any of us, Ted," she said, surprised at the lack of hatred in her voice. "It's been the worst time I've ever put in, and I think it's been the same for Mom and Dad. You just don't know what it's been like."

Slowly he looked up and their eyes met.

"Believe me, Connie, if there was anything in the world that I – that we could do to go back and change what happened, we would do it. We've all felt as though we had a terrible weight around our necks."

She twisted uncomfortably and looked down at her watch.

"I'm sorry, Ted, but I've got to go."

He stood quickly.

"Thanks for listening to me, Connie. I know how you feel about all of us, and I don't blame you. But I did want you to know how we feel about what happened."

Once Ted was gone Connie remained motionless in her chair for a minute. Emotion churned wildly within her. At the time she was talking with Ted she actually felt sorry for him. She knew his grief and wished there was something she could do to help him. After all, he wasn't responsible for what had happened any more than she had been.

But now that the conversation was over it was almost as though she had been disloyal to Fritz by talking to Ted Larson, if only for a moment. Her hands trembled and she knew there was no color in her cheeks.

Fritz wouldn't have wanted her to be angry with Ted Larson, or even Johnny, she had to acknowledge. He wouldn't have wanted her to stay away from church either. And there was nothing that would have disturbed him more than knowing she had turned her back on God.

But she couldn't help it. If God was a God of love, He would have kept her brother alive! Head swimming, she got to her feet and went back to work.

That night Connie was unable to sleep. But her wakefulness was not caused only by grief. It was the torment of her willfulness and sin in speaking out against God. Yet, how could she come back to Him when He had taken her only brother away? When He had allowed so much grief and heartache to come to her and to her parents?

She got up the next morning as tired as when she had gone to bed. All day long she could think of little else. Why had God taken Fritz? Why? Why? The question tormented her every waking moment.

Suddenly, the answer came, simply and straightforward.

Why not?

God had not spared His own Son when it suited His purpose to cause Him to die. Why should she think He should spare Fritz when his death would bring God honor and glory? Already the results of her brother's passing had been astonishing. More people than most Christians were able to lead to Christ in a lifetime had already received Him as Savior because of it.

And equally as many Christians who had drifted away from God had come back, repentant and sorrowing. And Fritz wasn't lost. Not really. God had just taken him home to be with Him. In that instant, all of Connie's bitterness and resentment fled. Tears coursed down her cheeks. Her supervisor saw that she was crying and came over to her quickly.

"Are you all right, Connie?" she asked, her voice tender.

Connie nodded.

"If you're feeling bad, you can take the rest of the afternoon off. We'll be able to manage without you." Connie shook her head. "That won't be necessary," she said. "I–I'm going to be fine now."

It seemed to her that the entire load of sorrow and hatred had been swept away.

The next few days at the office Connie worked quietly, unable to think of anything other than her new relationship with Christ. At first, she had felt a new peace and contentment, but that had only lasted a little while.

Even though the bitterness had evaporated, she still felt hollow and empty inside. She could tell that her parents sensed something new was troubling her, but she could not confide in them. At least, not until the matter was completely resolved in her own heart.

Every evening she took her Bible and tried to find comfort from it, but she could not seem to find any verses that would give her a great deal of help.

The approaching trial was bothering Connie more than she realized. It would come to mind at the most peculiar times. More than once she awakened at night thinking about it and unable to go back to sleep.

The night before Johnny's trial, Connie came home from work with a severe headache. She took some aspirin and lay down for a while.

Only a week before she had been so positive that she was going to be at the trial – that she was going to see the look on Johnny Larson's face when he was sentenced for manslaughter or for vehicular homicide. She had been positive that she wanted to see Johnny and his family hurt, just as he had hurt her and her parents.

But now she wasn't at all sure that she even wanted to be there. The Bible verse her dad quoted to her came back with a rush. *Vengeance is mine; I will repay, says the Lord.* She had gotten angry when he had quoted it. For a time she had even thought he could not have loved Fritz as much as he said he did and feel as he and Mom did. Now she saw the truth of it.

Connie was well aware that she would not be able to go to the trial. Not now. Not after she realized that she had the wrong attitude for a Christian. Not when she realized that she could not go there to get a measure of revenge. She couldn't go to see Johnny Larson punished.

Connie was not willing as yet to admit that God was working in her heart and life. Indeed, she was only vaguely aware of it – aware of the warmth of spirit that comes when one begins to move in a way that is pleasing to God. Full realization would come later. Now she was glad for the measure of release she had.

Connie went to work the day of Johnny's trial as though it were any other day. There were times that morning when she was still tempted to go to the trial, but forcibly she thought of something else. She wasn't going to let herself get upset the way she had been. Without quite realizing what was happening, she closed her eyes and began to pray silently.

She thought she would hear the outcome almost as soon as the trial was over, but there was no word until she got home that evening. Anxiously, she asked her dad about it.

"Johnny was granted a continuance in court this afternoon," he said. "The date of the trial has not been set, but Judge Abbott indicated it would be some time in October."

"That's a relief!"

Her parents both looked at her quizzically but made no comment. Connie, too, was surprised as she realized what she had said. But she honestly meant it. And in that moment, she was glad she did.

# CHAPTER 4

# RABBIT HUNTING

When Carmen Roper got home after taking the triplets north to live with Danny and Kay, she threw herself into her work furiously. She had found that if she worked until she was tired enough when she went to bed, she would be able to sleep, at least most of the night.

Clarence watched Phil closely and criticized him in ways he had never criticized him before. He refused to let him ask the blessing at the table and would explode with fury if he happened to catch his son reading his Bible or listening to a sermon.

Carmen did not know exactly when she started listening to religious programs or why. She had a feeling she did it out of admiration for Phil. He didn't lash back at his dad, although he had plenty of opportunity and reason for it, and he didn't weaken in his faith. He was as firm as the triplets or Rosalita and Jerry.

She couldn't help noticing the change that had come over him too. He had never been a bad boy. He took his share of the responsibilities about the ranch and seldom talked back. And he was cleaner talking than most of the boys his age. But now there was something very different about him. She couldn't quite understand what it was, but she did know that he had changed since he made this so-called decision for Christ. He was kinder and more considerate and seemed happier, in spite of the way Clarence treated him.

She even mentioned it to her husband.

"Different?" he echoed, cursing. "I'll say he's different. He doesn't have time to get into trouble. He sits around reading his Bible all the time."

"He is a good boy, Clarence," she retorted defensively. "You've got to give him credit for that."

"He's goody-goody. I'd rather have him like he was, any day. I hate to think what the guys will say when they find out what *my* son is like! It's a good thing we got rid of Rosalita's brats. If we hadn't, they'd have gotten to Marie too. Then we would have been in for a lot more trouble."

Carmen felt like crying, but she couldn't, not in front of Clarence. It would only make matters worse.

It wasn't long after that until she began to listen to the podcast that had first caused Phil to get interested in the triplets' religion. She felt guilty even putting it on and sat in her room with the door shut while she listened. And at night she would think about the things the preacher had said that day. There were times when they bothered her so much, she wasn't able to sleep at all and would turn sleeplessly in her bed until dawn.

But she secretively continued to listen. Only when the kids were in school and Clarence was gone did she dare to listen to the program aloud. Such occasions did not happen often, but when they did, she took full advantage of them.

This occasion was an example.

Clarence had gone to town on business earlier in the week and hadn't come back. The kids were home at night and for a little while in the morning, but they were at school for the rest of the day. That day Carmen had listened to the program twice, and what the speaker said was indelibly etched in her mind. Even when she went to bed, sleep was slow in coming. She tossed restlessly, staring up at the ceiling.

In the past Carmen had dreaded having Clarence away from home, even for a night. She dreaded being alone with the children in the big house. She dreaded the strange noises that always seemed to come at night when he wasn't there. She dreaded the responsibilities of the ranch, despite the fact that Clarence's foreman was a person who could be trusted implicitly to take care of every detail in exactly the way his employer wanted him to.

All of those things bothered Carmen as much now as they ever had. Yet, in spite of her fears, she was thankful that he would be away for a time. At least she would be able to listen to the programs without fear of being caught at it, and Phil would be able to read his Bible without running the risk of having his dad see him and upbraid him for it.

She rolled over on her side, and for a time was so disturbed she would have liked to get up. But she was afraid Phil or Marie would hear her and have questions they would want answered.

Why Clarence was so bitterly opposed to any of them listening to the program, she would never know. It wasn't costing him anything. It couldn't even hurt his pride because she would never let anyone know she was a listener. There had to be another reason.

She suspected it was because he was afraid of what was being preached and didn't want any of the other members of the family to come under the influence of the gospel. But he didn't have to be afraid of what was preached. The speakers certainly weren't such spellbinders that they'd talk her, or anyone else, into doing something they didn't want to do.

Carmen breathed deeply. No, she wasn't going to be carried away by what those men preached. She had seen enough of that sort of thing in her sister Rosalita and that husband of hers, who dragged her off to some horrible place where they both got themselves killed.

"To preach the gospel," they said – as though that made sense.

Carmen sat up in bed, her eyes wide and staring.

Why she listened to the programs so regularly, she did not know. She had never done anything that had made her feel so unworthy – so miserable. More than once after listening to the program she had tossed sleeplessly all night long – as she was doing right now – with something the speaker had said racing through her mind.

> *All have sinned, and come short of the*
> *glory of God. There is none righteous, no,*
> *not one. The wages of sin is death.*

Why did it have to keep hammering at her until she felt as though she was the most vile, wicked person in the world?

Her lips were quivering.

When Rosalita and her husband died, they went to heaven. Even Carmen had to admit that was true. If she were to die now – this very night – what would happen to her?

* * *

Doug and Del Davis counted the days until their

Saturday rabbit-hunting expedition with Hank Blair and Danny. On Friday night before the basketball game, they got out some heavy clothes, cleaned the rifles for the third time that week, and talked with Kay about lunch. DeeDee came into the kitchen while they were discussing the matter.

"What are you going to do?" she asked curiously.

"Haven't you heard?" Doug grinned at her. "Danny is taking us rabbit hunting."

"You aren't really going rabbit hunting, are you?" she asked.

"Sure we are," Del replied. "Did I hear you say you'd like to go along?"

DeeDee shuddered. She had an idea they were teasing her, but the thought of hunting was more than she could bear.

"Go along?" she echoed. "I wouldn't go along and watch you kill those poor, innocent little rabbits for a thousand dollars." Her eyes sparked. "I hope you don't get any. I hope you don't even *see* any."

"Well, that's just tough," Del retorted. "You don't know how good we are when it comes to hunting. We're not only going to get a couple of nice, fat rabbits apiece, but we're goin' to skin them and fry them for supper."

DeeDee made a horrible face.

"Del!" she exclaimed. "Don't talk that way! I get sick just thinking about it."

Doug broke in.

"I'll bet it would be different if Tim Porter was going rabbit hunting. I can just hear you, 'Oh, Tim, you're so brave going after those ferocious rabbits. And with a little .22!'" He sighed in exaggerated awe. "'You must be the bravest hunter in the whole world!'"

Flushing scarlet, DeeDee turned and left the room.

* * *

It was still dark when Hank Blair drove up to the Orlis house and honked, but Danny and the boys had been ready for half an hour and were waiting for him. They hurried out to the car and piled in.

"How far is this place you're taking us to?" Danny asked.

"It isn't very far," Hank replied mysteriously. "In fact, you could say that it's quite close to town."

He turned north on the highway and drove to the first turn beyond the river bridge. He went west a short distance and turned north once more. As he drove, he talked continuously.

"This place is close to town, Danny, but it's a beautiful spot. One of the prettiest I've seen in either Minnesota or Ontario." He glanced obliquely at his missionary companion. "And both the mail and the school bus go by the lane. The kids would only have to walk a quarter of a mile out to the mailbox to catch the bus to school."

Danny frowned.

"I thought you said there's nobody living on the farm."

"There isn't."

"Then, what's this about kids only having to walk a quarter of a mile to catch a bus to school?"

Mr. Blair acted as though he hadn't even heard what Danny said.

In the bleak, gray early morning light, the countryside was beautiful. Some of the land was second-growth timber, but some looked as though it has never been logged. Norway pines stretched their tousled heads toward the sky, towering far above the birch and the poplar.

"I fell in love with this spot the first time I saw it," the businessman continued. "I only wish my job made it possible for me to move my family out here."

"It's beautiful, that's for sure."

Mr. Blair pulled up before a low, rambling ranch house that was almost new.

"It's a shame to have a place like this vacant, wouldn't you say?"

Danny nodded.

"I have to confess something, Danny," he went on. "I had something more than rabbit hunting in mind when I invited you and the boys to come out here."

Danny stared at his host in bewilderment. "You've really got me confused now," he said. "I don't get this at all."

Hank grinned crookedly and his lips parted as

though he was about to reply. Instead, however, he opened the car door and got out.

"Danny, I'd like to show you around the house to see what you think of it."

"It looks beautiful from here."

"My wife, Nancy, is just crazy about it."

Only Del hung back. "Wait a minute," he exclaimed. "Aren't we going rabbit hunting?"

"In a little while." Mr. Blair opened the kitchen door and ushered Danny and the boys inside the vacant house. The kitchen was large and airy. There was tile on the floor and a built-in stove. An almost new refrigerator stood in one corner.

"Beautiful, isn't it?" he asked.

"It sure is," Danny said. "I don't think I've ever been in a more inviting kitchen."

"That's exactly the way I feel about it." He walked around, pulling open cupboard doors and peering into them. "It sort of makes a guy wish there was some furniture in it so he could sit down and have a cup of coffee."

Danny reached down and felt the register. Warm air was coming out of it.

"We've left the furnace on to keep the pipes from freezing."

"How long has the place been empty?"

"A month or so, I guess. I'm not exactly sure when the former owner moved out."

With that he led them into the living room.

"Take a look at that fireplace. There isn't a more attractive fireplace in all of Minnesota."

Danny nodded. He didn't think he had ever seen a fireplace the equal of the one he was now looking at.

"And take a squint at the lake out the picture window," Blair continued. "A person couldn't ask for anything more, now could he?"

Danny whistled. "You can say that again."

"That's just what I wanted to hear from you." Hank pivoted to face him. "Well, how would you like to live here?"

Danny's eyes widened. "I guess you know the answer to that one without even asking. But you forget that I'm a missionary. We don't get enough support money to make it possible for us to even think about living in a house like this."

Hank smiled. "I didn't ask if you could afford it, Danny," he said. "I asked if you'd like to live here."

"Who wouldn't want to live here, if he could?"

"Then, it's settled. It's yours."

Danny was slow in understanding him. "I'm sure you don't mean what I think you said, Hank," he replied.

His companion laughed. "If you thought I meant that you can live here rent-free, you're right. That's exactly what I meant."

Danny's eyes narrowed thoughtfully. "But why?"

"Ever since Nancy and I saw this house we decided that it would be ideal for you and Kay and the triplets, so I started working on our company president. I got word last week that you can live in the house rent-free for keeping the place in good repair."

For a time Danny could not answer him.

## CHAPTER 5

# THE HOUSE

It was almost dawn before Carmen Roper was finally able to go to sleep. Even then she slept lightly, and in a little while she wakened, an icy heaviness weighing on her. At first she only knew that she was disturbed about something. She wasn't able to determine what it was. Gradually she began to remember. Her mind went back to the thoughts that had troubled her so much during the night.

> *The wages of sin is death. . . . The wages of sin is death. . . .*

That portion of the Bible verse the speaker had quoted the day before kept going over and over in her mind. Grimly she tried to force it out of her mind and go back to sleep, but she could not. The truth of those words kept hammering at her.

49

Although she slept no more, she did not get up until it was time to get breakfast for Marie and Phil and see that they were off to school. When she finished dressing and went to the kitchen, Marie was already dressed and sitting at the table drinking a glass of milk.

"Well now, I didn't expect to see you up so soon," Carmen exclaimed brightly, hiding her feelings of frustration and bewilderment with a smile. "What caused this?"

"Hi, Mom." Marie glanced at her impishly. "I got out of bed before you did this morning."

"So I see."

"I got to thinking about Dad coming home," she said, "and I got so excited I couldn't sleep, so I got up and dressed."

Carmen put the coffeepot on the front burner of her propane stove.

"You won't be able to see Dad until you get home from school tonight," she said. "And even then, he might not make it."

"I hope he does. I don't like it when he's away. It–it's sort of scary."

Carmen nodded. "I don't like it either," she answered.

In the silence that followed the Bible verse continued to scream at her, *The wages of sin is death – The wages of sin is death*. That meant they were all sinners – Clarence, Carmen, Marie, and everyone else.

But in their family, only Philip had done anything about it. If he died, he would go to heaven, but he was the only one in the family who would. The rest of them were lost.

Carmen started talking rapidly to her daughter, making observations, asking questions, anything to keep from having to think.

After a time Phil joined them for breakfast. He was dressed in a pair of old jeans and boots.

"Aren't you going to school today?" his mother asked.

"If Dad'll be home today, I'd better ride that fence he told me to check. He's going to be awfully mad if he comes home and finds that it isn't done."

His mother nodded. "He's going to be mad if he finds that you haven't been to school today too."

Phil's gaze met hers. "I suppose you're right about that, but it's the only time I've had to take care of it."

"I'm sure Dad forgot that you're in school, Philip," Carmen said. "I'll talk to him when he gets back. It would be better for you to ride the fence Saturday."

As soon as breakfast was over, he went back to his room and changed clothes. Marie waited impatiently for him in the kitchen.

"Hurry up, Phil!" she sang out. "We're going to miss the bus if you don't!"

He came out buttoning his shirt.

"Okay. Okay," he said. "I'm ready."

Then they were gone, and Carmen was alone in

the sprawling ranch house. She had told herself she wasn't going to listen to the preacher that morning. She was already upset enough without hearing any more sermons. She'd saddle a horse and go out and ride the fence herself. Clarence didn't like to have her do things like that, and usually she didn't, but she enjoyed getting out once in a while.

She started for the bedroom to change clothes. The clock chimed and she counted the notes mechanically.

Nine o'clock.

Carmen stopped short. That was the time the preacher came on live in the morning. He could be heard later, but she had been listening in the morning if she could. There was usually less chance of having Clarence catch her at it then.

For half a minute she hesitated. It wouldn't hurt to listen to the music, she reasoned. It was always so beautiful. And there wouldn't be any preaching until after several songs. She was still determined not to listen to the speaker. That was what caused her the trouble.

She turned back to the living room and sat down. The familiar strains of the religious program's theme song filled the room.

Almost immediately, Carmen realized that she should not have sat down and turned on the podcast. She just might not be able to turn it off when the music was over. That had happened to her on other occasions.

Her hand shot out to turn it off, but with her fingers on the button, she stopped. Why, she didn't know. She didn't want to listen. Yet something – or someone compelled her to do so.

The speaker was talking about missions that morning, but he also spoke about God and His great love for sinners.

Carmen was thrilled as she listened. This was something she hadn't fully realized before. God loved her. He actually loved Carmen Roper! He knew all the sinful things she had done. He knew the blackness of her heart. He knew she made fun of those who loved Him and that she didn't want to have anything to do with Him. But in spite of all of that, He loved her so much that He sent the Lord Jesus Christ to die on the cross to save her from the results of her sin.

Carmen was crying now, but she was crying tears of joy. The wages of sin was death, she realized. That still had not been changed. But she didn't have to pay those wages because Christ had already paid them with His spotless life. She slipped quietly to her knees while the speaker was still talking and asked God to forgive her sin and to take full and complete control of her life.

It was a long while before she got to her feet. A new radiance seemed to envelop her. She had a joy and a peace she had never known before. It was as though she had suddenly become a new person.

Slowly a new revelation came to her, knifing to

the very depths of her being. What about Clarence? He had been so furious when he learned what had taken place in Phil's life that he made the triplets go somewhere else to live. He would have placed them in a children's home rather than have them in his own house. What would he say when he found out that she was a Christian now?

Her blood chilled.

What would he do when he found out that there were two believers in his family, instead of just one?

* * *

Like Danny, Kay was astonished when she heard about Hank's offer to let them live in the beautiful ranch-style home rent free. At first she thought Danny was teasing her when he described it, but one look at his face told her that he wasn't.

"You do mean it, don't you?" she asked, after a moment or two.

"I sure do." He was so excited about it the words tumbled out. "And wait until you see it. You'll say that it's one of the nicest houses you've ever been in."

"It sounds too good to be true."

"But it isn't," Del put in. "You just ought to go out with us and see it. It's super."

"It sure is," Doug added. "And when the ice goes out, there's going to be amazing fishing right at our back door. Imagine that!"

They drove out to the house that afternoon and went through it. Kay found the house even nicer than she had supposed it would be. She hadn't expected it to be in such good repair or to have so many closets and built-in cupboards.

"I've always dreamed about a house like this," she said, "but I never thought we'd have a chance to live in one."

DeeDee was even more excited than Kay if that were possible. She had already picked out one of the bedrooms as her own. She didn't choose the biggest or the nicest. She figured it should belong to Danny and Kay. But there was no reason why she shouldn't get her pick next, she told herself. Boys didn't care much what their rooms were like and especially a couple like Del and Doug. They didn't pay much attention to nice things anyway.

She had always wanted a nice room of her own. One with a good floor and attractive walls. A room that she could fix any way she wanted to.

She talked with Danny and Kay about it on the way home.

"Why should she get her pick?" Del protested. "There are two of us. We ought to get the biggest."

"They're both the same size," Danny reminded him.

"Why don't we draw straws?" Doug suggested. "The shortest straw gets first pick."

But Danny did not go along with that. "DeeDee

asked about it first," he said. "I think she should have first choice."

The boys fussed a little about the decision, but they weren't greatly disturbed by it. They just wanted to file a protest in case DeeDee took advantage of this gain or tried to. They had served notice that they were not going to let her get away with getting preferred treatment if they could help it.

Danny and Kay and the triplets went out to the new house several times in the week that followed. Kay checked all of the windows to see if her curtains and drapes would fit. And in the afternoon, when she was home alone, she sketched out plans of each room and drew in the furniture in the arrangement she thought she would like best.

They had planned on moving the first of the month, but an unseasonable blizzard snarled out of the north, piling drifts high on the roads. Reluctantly they decided to wait for another week.

DeeDee was terribly disappointed and asked Danny, "Do you think the storm will stop so we can move tomorrow?"

"I'm afraid there's no chance of that." He looked out the window at the drifting snow. "The weather bureau says this storm may last several days."

Doug broke in. "Besides, DeeDee–" he said, the superiority of the all-wise male in his voice, "even if the storm did stop, the snowplows wouldn't have the roads opened up by tomorrow. Nope, we're stuck here for a while. We're not going to be able to move until this is over."

She was crestfallen, but only for an instant or two. "I'm going to pray that God will stop the storm and help the men on the snowplows get the road open so we can move."

Del studied her young face momentarily, a strange look twisting his mouth.

"You don't expect God to answer a prayer like that, do you?" he scoffed.

"I certainly do."

Danny caught the tone of doubt in his voice. Later he and Kay talked about it.

"Did you hear what Del said about DeeDee's decision to pray?" he asked.

She nodded. "It wasn't his words as much as the tone of his voice that bothered me," she replied.

"I felt the same way. It was almost as though he doesn't believe in prayer or would like to make himself believe that he doesn't."

There was a short silence.

"I was watching him in church last Sunday," she went on. "You know, he used to pay close attention to the entire service, but Sunday he was fooling around instead of listening. I had to talk to him about it when we got home."

"I'll have to watch him a little more closely next Sunday. It may be that bunch of guys he was sitting with."

The next morning when they got up, the storm was over, and the day dawned bright and clear. DeeDee accepted the fact without surprise and with complete faith that prayer had stopped the wind and snow and had driven the clouds away.

"See, Del," she said. "It's nice outside this morning. The snowplows won't have any trouble opening the roads now. We'll still be able to move."

Her brother had nothing to say.

That afternoon the road was plowed open, and after school the boys and Danny hauled two loads of furniture to the country before dark. The next morning they finished the job.

In the big, new home DeeDee glanced about appraisingly and turned to Kay. "I don't think there's a nicer house anywhere in Minnesota," she said.

Tears came up into Kay's eyes and trickled unashamedly down her cheeks. She had never thought they would have such a lovely home. God had been so good to them.

# CHAPTER 6

# TEXAS TROUBLE

Clarence Roper came home late that afternoon as he had planned. He jumped out of the car and came striding up to the house in steps that no one else on the ranch could have taken.

"Carmen!" he called out as he went up the back steps and into the kitchen. "Carmen!"

"In here," she replied. In spite of her joy at having him home, apprehension caused her voice to quaver slightly as she answered him. But he did not notice. He came bounding in where she was and swept her into his arms.

"Everything worked out perfectly, Carmen." His great voice boomed throughout the house.

"Th-th-that's nice," she managed to say. "And I'm so glad you're home. We all are."

"I got a much better price for the cattle than I even dreamed was possible," he told her excitedly. "And the way it looks we may be able to contract to sell next year's calves to the same buyer at a nice premium."

He released her from his powerful embrace and went over to a chair and sat down.

"You should have heard them, Carmen," he continued. "You'd have been proud of the Circle R. They said our stock is worth a higher price. They said a lot of cattle feeders are wanting Circle R calves because they're healthier and make better market animals."

"That–that's wonderful!"

"I'll say it is!" He went over and kissed her again. "I was wishing you were along so we could take in a few night spots to celebrate."

She did not answer him. All of this was good news. She was happy for Clarence. He worked hard and there was no doubt that he was one of the best cattlemen in the territory. Other ranchers were always coming to him with their problems, and most of the time he had the answers for them.

But that new uneasiness nagged at her. None of these things were going to help when he found out that she had decided to risk his anger and make her decision for Christ.

What would he do? The question drove its barbs deep within her.

After dinner that evening when the children were studying in their rooms, Clarence turned to his wife.

"You sure are quiet tonight," he said, the hurt

evident in his voice. "You don't act very happy about the sale of our cattle."

"Oh, I am." She forced a razor-thin smile. "I'm not only happy, but I'm also proud of you, Clarence. It's because you're the best cattleman in this part of Texas that you get the sort of prices you do. Everybody tells me that, and I'm very proud of you."

His expansive smile came once more. "That's better," he said. "That's a lot better."

She knew that he was excited and happy and wanted her to be the same way, but every time she tried to smile, she thought of what had happened to her while her husband was gone. That happiness of his would fade in an instant if he found out.

After a time he sensed her uneasiness once more and his smile faded.

"Carmen," he said, "what's the matter? What's wrong?"

It was all she could do to lift her gaze to meet his.

"Is–is there something wrong?" she asked, trying to sound light and frivolous to match his mood. But, even as she spoke, she knew that it didn't come off very well. "I feel fine."

He went over and took hold of her shoulders. "Listen, Carmen," he said, his voice grating. "I've lived with you for a good many years. I know whether there's something wrong or not. And there's something bothering you tonight." He paused. "In fact, there's something been bothering you ever since I got home. I'd like to know what it is."

"Well, there isn't anything wrong. Believe me."

The words seemed to burn her lips as they came out. There was something wrong, and she knew what it was. Only she couldn't voice it – not when it could mean the end of everything between them!

There was a long, pained silence. Carmen fought desperately for control of herself. She couldn't stand to look at Clarence, but she could not keep from it. Her husband was staring evenly into her eyes.

"Carmen," he began again, his voice quietly insistent. "Carmen, is there something wrong? Did something happen while I was away that I ought to know about?"

She shook her head. "No," she replied. "Everything went fine."

"You're sure?"

She hesitated. How could she tell him that she had accepted Christ as her Savior when she knew how bitterly he hated the gospel? He might ask her to leave or force her to choose between her newly-found faith and him and the kids. How could she tell him what had happened when it could well mean the end of everything for her?

For an instant, but only for an instant, she wished she had never heard the gospel. At least she wouldn't be faced with this problem if she hadn't. On the other hand, she would only have a Christless eternity to look forward to if she hadn't become a Christian. She could never turn her back on God, no matter what Clarence did or threatened to do.

"N-nothing happened that you ought to know about, Clarence," she repeated. "Don't you believe me?"

His mouth tightened. "You don't usually lie to me," he said, "so if you tell me there's nothing wrong, I've got to believe you. But I can tell you this much, Carmen, you sure act suspicious to me. Right now, you act as though you're trying to carry the whole world on your shoulders and you're afraid that it's going to slip off."

Her gaze searched his. "Th-th-there's nothing wrong." Although she managed to smile, she was actually very close to tears.

He leaned over impulsively and kissed her.

"Okay. Let's forget about that. I'm too excited and happy tonight to be upset anyway." He took a deep breath. "I sure wish you'd been with me. We'd have done some high-class celebrating before we came home."

Carmen tried in desperation to match the happiness of his mood, but the ache in her heart continued to grow. She had not been a Christian more than twenty-four hours and already she was lying. What was the matter with her anyway?

At that instant she was so miserable that had Clarence questioned her further, she would have blurted the truth. But he was so talkative he didn't even notice that she was more pensive and quieter than before. He told her again, in full detail, everything that had happened when he was in town – what he had said to the buyer and what the buyer had said to him. She only half listened, murmuring her assent at the proper times.

Late that night, in the quiet of the bedroom, Carmen lay motionless, her mind racing. She couldn't tell Clarence that she was a Christian. She loved him too much to risk that. Yet, she could not continue to deceive him. She couldn't let him go on thinking that she was the same as she had always been. She had to tell him the truth.

It wasn't going to be easy, she knew. She would have to confess to him that she had lied to him for the first time since they had been married. Silently Carmen began to pray.

Although she knew she was going to have to tell him the truth she kept postponing it for one reason or another. First she wanted to catch him when he was in the right mood. Then it would have to be when the kids were in school or away far enough so there was no danger of them coming back and getting in on the middle of everything. After that, she put it off because she was afraid one of the men or the foreman would come to the door and knock while they were talking.

All the while, she was listening to the preacher every day. Strangely enough, he was having a series of messages on living a holy and set apart Christian life. He emphasized again and again that a believer had to come clean for God. He quoted one Bible verse after another that showed a Christian had to turn every avenue of his life over to the Lord Jesus Christ if he expected God to work in his life.

Carmen reasoned defensively that she had done that. She had turned all of her life over to God. She had quit doing those things she knew to be sin. She read her Bible every day and even had a time of prayer. And seldom did she let a day go by without listening to the preacher, at least once.

Yet, even as she tried to defend her actions by recounting her new virtues, remorse stabbed at her. It wasn't true that she had come clean for God. Not really. She hadn't come clean with her husband. She hadn't called him aside and confessed that she was a Christian. Instead, she had done everything she could to keep him from finding out the truth. She kept her Bible hidden in the bottom of a drawer where he would never look and waited until she was sure he was away from the buildings before she got it out to read.

One of the reasons she was glad the message was recorded each day was so she would have a chance to hear it in the afternoon if Clarence was in the house at nine in the morning. And if her husband made a remark about Philip's faith or his Bible reading or prayer, she either agreed with him or remained silent.

No, she hadn't come clean with Clarence. Painfully, she had to admit that.

Conviction stabbed at Carmen until she could not sleep. She even had difficulty in going to God in prayer. For all of the joy that being a Christian had brought her, she had to recognize that she had been living a lie ever since she confessed her sin and turned her life over to Christ.

Finally she knew what she had to do. Indeed, she had known it all along, but had been avoiding it on one pretense or another.

Carmen got up almost an hour earlier than usual that morning and spent the extra time on her knees. Clarence was in no hurry in getting out to work that morning and lingered at the table over a cup of coffee until Phil and Marie had gone out to wait for the school bus.

"Well," he said at last, pushing away from the table. "I guess I'd better get out and see how those new calves are doing."

He would have left, but Carmen laid a trembling hand on his arm.

"I'd like to talk to you, Clarence," she said.

He eyed her curiously. "If there's something you want to buy, go ahead and get it. You know that you don't have to ask me about things like that."

She shook her head. "It isn't that."

Nevertheless, he got to his feet impatiently. He seemed as anxious now to avoid talking to her as he had been to talk with her about the thing that was troubling her a few nights before.

"Can it wait, Carmen? I've got a lot of work to do."

Suddenly all her frustration and anguish welled within her, and she was impatient to speak.

"That's the trouble," she blurted. "I've waited too long already."

He saw the concern in her eyes and, pulling up a chair, sat down beside her.

"Now, what's the trouble?" he asked, his voice tender. "What is it that's got you all worked up?"

"I–" She swallowed hard. "I–"

"You don't have to be afraid to tell me anything, Carmen. You ought to know that by this time."

She reached out and laid her hand on his gnarled fingers. He was a good man in spite of his rough, blustery ways. And she loved him dearly.

For an instant she faltered, wondering what would happen when she told him. But she couldn't stop now. He had a right to know.

"Clarence, I–" She swallowed against the lump in her throat. "Clarence, I'm a Christian now. I–"

He stared at her incredulously, eyes widening. Anger twisted his face.

"Carmen!" he cried. "Don't joke about that! You hear me?"

She was trembling violently. "I'm not joking." The sound of her voice seemed to steady her somewhat.

"It's the truth, Clarence," she repeated. "I'm a Christian now."

He stared numbly at her. The color seeped from his cheeks, leaving them ashen, and rage gleamed in his eyes. He grasped the kitchen table on either side, and his grip tightened until the cords stood out on the back of his powerful hands. He seemed transfixed by the information that his wife named Christ as her Savior. His shoulders jerked spasmodically, as though he was suddenly seized with convulsions.

With a quick movement he pushed away from the table, knocking over his chair as he did so. For a tense half minute, he glared down at Carmen, his hand quivering as though he was undecided whether to slap her or just walk away. At last he whirled and stormed outside.

She stared after him miserably until she was sure he was gone. Then she buried her head in her arms on the kitchen table and began to sob. Clarence was gone. Everything between them was over now!

# CHAPTER 7

# ANIMAL PICTURES

The Davis triplets were more excited about living on the farm with each passing day. Doug and Del could scarcely wait for the school bus to get them home in the afternoons after school. And on Saturdays they always had some sort of a project going. They raked the yard, repaired the roof of an old granary, and cleaned out the barn. They checked over their fishing tackle and helped Danny put another coat of paint on the boat.

At last all the work was done and for the first time since they moved, they had an entire Saturday with nothing to do. They lay on their backs in the haymow staring idly up at the cobwebs.

Del spoke first. "I sure wish we were down in Texas on the ranch this afternoon," he said wistfully. "We could go for a ride on our horses."

"Yeah," Doug said, "if Uncle Clarence was over

being mad at us. The way he was when we left, he'd never let us get close to that ranch."

"I forgot all about that."

"I haven't." Doug shuddered. "I can still see him glaring at us. I thought he was going to beat us half to death."

They talked about the ranch for a while, wondering how Phil was getting along in his Christian life and what Marie and Aunt Carmen were doing. While they were talking, a car drove by. Doug waited until the sound died away before he spoke once more.

"I sure wish there was something else to do around here."

"We could go for a boat ride," his brother suggested.

"Who wants to put the boat in the water and hook up the outboard and everything?" Doug asked.

Del sat up quickly. "I just thought of something," he exclaimed. "I've been wanting to use that camera I got for Christmas, but I haven't done much except take a few shots around the house. Why don't we go out and see if we can get some animal pictures? Okay?"

Doug got to his feet and dusted off his pants. Taking pictures didn't sound very exciting to him, but it was better than lying in the haymow with nothing to do.

"Sounds all right to me."

They went up to the house to get Del's new camera. When they reached the living room, DeeDee was sprawled on the floor studying. She too had been trying to think of something to do. As soon as she saw her brothers she scrambled to her feet.

"Where're you going?"

Doug shrugged. "I don't know for sure. We're just going out and mess around for a while."

"Can I go along?"

Her brother hesitated. "We might go quite a ways," he told her. "Maybe even down to the end of the lake and back."

"That's not so far."

"You'd get tired."

Defiance flashed in her dark eyes.

"I can tell you this much, Doug Davis," she flared, "I can walk just as far as you and Del can and never complain or have to stop to rest. That's for sure."

"There are a lot of mosquitoes now," he said. "The last time we were down that way they almost ate us up."

She straightened indignantly.

"You're just trying to talk me out of going with you. That's what you're trying to do. The mosquitoes aren't half as bad here as they used to be in Guatemala."

He paused. "Well–"

"And besides, Kay's got some new insect repellent that's perfect. If you put some of it on, it'll keep the mosquitoes away for hours."

"Who says so?"

"I've tried it."

Doug sighed. He knew when he was licked.

Next Del tried his hand at discouraging DeeDee, but he was no more successful than Doug had been. In the end he also agreed to let her go. He got his camera and the three of them left the buildings and angled across a narrow meadow to a path fifty yards or so from the lake.

"Let me go first." Del pushed by his sister. "I want to be where I can get a good picture in case we see any game."

DeeDee started to protest, but checked herself when she saw that his request was reasonable. Obediently she fell in line behind him.

"And whatever you do, be quiet, DeeDee," Del warned. "One little squeak out of you and any animals in the area will be gone."

"Why don't you talk to Doug?" she demanded irritably. "Why am I the one you have to warn about everything? I won't cause as much noise as either of you two."

Doug spoke up. "That's what you think. Girls don't know enough to be quiet. That's why a boy has to keep telling them all the time."

DeeDee snorted indignantly. "I don't see why I couldn't have had just one sister," she complained. "I don't see why my brothers both had to be boys."

Del stopped suddenly, head cocked to one side, listening. But whatever it was that had been in the woods ahead, it was gone now. He couldn't hear it anymore. He turned to his sister.

"See, what'd I tell you? You're going to scare every animal out of the woods if you keep up that jabbering."

"Me?" Her voice rose. "You're both talking a blue streak, and that's all right. You can say anything you want to, as loudly as you want to, but that won't scare anything. But if I say something, you act as though I've committed a crime or something."

"You were the one who scared him away."

"I'm almost sorry I came along with you," she snorted in indignation.

"You can always turn around and go back if you're sorry you're with us. It won't make us feel bad."

She stared at him.

"I'm not *that* sorry!"

The boys both laughed.

"You don't have to get so mad at us," he said. "We were just having a little fun with you."

When she saw that they were only teasing her, she relaxed slightly, her cheeks flushing.

"Oh, you two!" she exclaimed. "You make me so mad!"

They went on up the narrow, winding trail. The forest closed in so close on either side that the brush touched their shoulders and the trees blotted out the sun. Here and there they had to clamber over a dead fall or a poplar the wind had blown over.

Del, who was still leading the trio, stopped suddenly, eyes widening. DeeDee and Doug came up beside him.

"What is it?" DeeDee whispered.

For answer he pointed at the huge black stain on the ferns and grass. DeeDee spoke once more, curiously.

"What is it?" she asked again.

"Somebody killed an animal here and dressed it out."

Doug nodded. "That must be what it is. That's dried blood, all right."

Del squatted to examine the ground more carefully. However, it was DeeDee who found the tuft of hair that identified the animal.

"Look at this!" she exclaimed.

Del took it from her and held it up where the light was better.

"I know what it's from. It's the hair of a deer," Doug told him.

"It is, for a fact! Some poacher must have killed him."

Horror widened DeeDee's eyes. "I don't see how anyone could do a thing like that. Those poor, innocent little deer."

Del put the tuft of hair in his pocket. "I'm going to see that the game warden gets this. He ought to know what's been going on out here so he can keep an eye on the place."

There was a brief silence. At last Doug spoke up. "What're we going to do now?"

"I'd about as soon turn around and go back to the house," Del said. The life had gone out of his voice. "Something like this makes me sick. I don't feel much like going any farther."

"Neither do I," DeeDee added.

As they turned around Del heard a faint rustling sound in the brush. He jerked to a halt, his voice lowering.

"Wh-what was that?" he demanded.

"I didn't hear anything."

It came again – so faintly he couldn't be entirely sure there was anything there. Yet there had to be! He glanced about. DeeDee's face was ashen, and his brother Doug was breathing heavily.

Maybe the poachers had come back for something! Maybe they had heard him say he was going to turn them in to the game warden!

Del's blood chilled.

* * *

Carmen Roper worked mechanically around the house the rest of the day. It was as though she was only half alive – that something terrible had happened to leave her just a shell of what she had been before.

In all the time they had been married, she had never known Clarence to get so angry with her. She had never seen such rage in his eyes. At the moment she didn't know whether he would ever come back.

Carmen had heard her sister Rosalita tell about homes in Guatemala that were broken by the gospel, homes where either the husband or wife would make a decision for Christ and find that his marriage was broken because of it. Somehow, when Rosalita talked, those things had never seemed particularly real to her. She believed her sister, all right, but it was almost as though she had not been talking about real people.

Now her mind went back to those incidents with a rush. It could well be that she would find herself in a similar situation.

At first Carmen prayed as she went through the motions of running the sweeper and dusting, but as the hours passed and Clarence did not return, it seemed that she lacked the strength even for that. She had known all along that she loved her husband, but until now she hadn't realized exactly how much he meant to her. They had been married so many years she had been taking him for granted, assuming that he would always love her, and they would stay together. Now all of her security was gone. There was a good chance that she would lose him.

As noon approached, Carmen's hopes flickered briefly. There was a chance that he might come home at noon. With growing tension, she watched the clock, hope mounting on hope that he would come striding in as though nothing had happened. But he did not show up.

Numbly Carmen made lunch and set the table for herself. That evening Clarence still had not come back. By this time Carmen was sure that he had gone for good.

Phil and Marie knew there was something wrong as soon as they got home from school. They saw it written on Carmen's face and in the listless way she went about her work. They found an excuse to be in and out of the house often, and when they came to the table their eyes reflected their concern.

Phil looked about uneasily.

"Where's Dad?" he asked.

Carmen busied herself at the stove.

"You know how it is with him. He's always got a dozen things to do."

But her son was not satisfied. "He acted awful mad about something when he left the house this morning. At least that's what one of the men told me."

Carmen felt her eyes flood with tears. She winked them back determinedly. Although she could control the outward signs of crying, she was sobbing within.

"Buck told me Dad had him saddle his horse this morning and then he took off, just like that. Said he'd never seen him ride Gentleman Joe so hard."

Carmen did not reply immediately. At least she knew he went off on a horse. She felt a little better about that. If he had been going to leave for good, he probably would have taken the car.

"I–I'm sure he'll be back before long."

She tried hard to keep her fear from showing in her voice. The fact that Clarence had ridden off on his cow horse didn't mean that he had not decided to leave. This, she knew. He wasn't one to change easily. He could be riding across the prairie trying to think, trying to decide whether to make her leave or whether to leave himself.

When they had finished eating and Clarence still had not shown up, Marie asked about her dad. She, too, was uneasy.

"He sure must have had a lot to do," she said, "or he'd be home by this time."

"The way he took off," Phil exclaimed, "he was either awful mad or awful worried about something. The guys are still talkin' about it."

Carmen looked away quickly. She couldn't bring herself to tell the children just yet. Not until she knew for sure. She prayed silently for strength and courage to face whatever God had in store for her.

Phil and Marie went to bed at the usual time, and Carmen went into the living room alone. Her Bible was on the end table. Numbly she picked it up and began to thumb its crisp, clean pages. Although they had had it for a long while – it had been a gift from Rosalita and Jerry the first year after they were married – it had been used little.

Carmen was still looking at it, her mind unable to focus on the words, when the front door opened. She looked up.

There stood Clarence, wide-eyed and staring. His lips trembled. She tried to speak to him, but for the moment, she could not.

# CHAPTER 8

# POOR LITTLE GUY

For half a minute the Davis triplets remained motionless, staring into the brush around them. The sound came again – a thin, rustling noise that had an air of stealth about it. At last Del found his voice.

"Wh-wh-what do you suppose it is?"

Doug glanced frantically over his shoulder, as though the wisest course was to take flight immediately.

"I don't know," he retorted, "and I don't care much whether we find out or not. I think we'd better get out of here."

DeeDee whispered firmly. "It–it's anything that's going to hurt us, it would have done it a long time ago."

Del had to admit that sounded logical. He had never had any experience with poachers, but he didn't think they would hang around a place making a noise. They'd do what they were going to do or hide or get out of there.

DeeDee parted the thick undergrowth and peered down. A gasp escaped her lips. The boys stared at her.

"What is it?" Doug demanded.

She did not answer his question.

"Oh, the poor little thing!"

By this time both Doug and Del were staring over her shoulders, startled by what they saw. Del caught his breath. "A fawn!"

"It's been wounded!" Doug cried. "Look at that arrow!"

At the sound of their voices, the frightened little animal struggled to stand, but it could not. Its eyes were rolled back in terror, and its frail body shook violently. DeeDee reached out her hand to touch it, but it shrank away. That only made her feel sorrier for him.

"The poor little thing is so scared he doesn't even want anyone to touch him," she murmured.

Del pushed up beside his sister and knelt in the grass and ferns.

"There now, we're not going to hurt you."

His voice was gentle and soothing as he talked to the frightened little animal. He talked to the fawn in low tones but made no attempt to touch him. As his voice continued without any actions that looked as though he might hurt the little deer, the fawn seemed to sense that he was safe. He stopped trembling, except for a moment after Del laid his hand tenderly on him. At that there was a brief spasm of fear. Del did not move his hand but quieted the deer under the caressing tone of his voice.

"That's all right," he said softly. "We're not going to hurt you. You don't have to be afraid of us."

"The poor little guy." Doug eyed the arrow protruding from the animal's hip. "I'd like to get my hands on the character who shot him!"

"So would I. He ought to have something like this happen to him once or twice. Then he'd know what it's like."

DeeDee straightened and looked around, as though she had just thought of something.

"What do you think happened?" she asked. "Do you suppose the poachers shot both the mother and the fawn with arrows and then couldn't find the baby?"

Del nodded, his eyes flashing their anger.

"I'm sure they killed the doe, all right. That's the only possible explanation for all the blood and deer hair. But they didn't look for the fawn. They didn't even try to find him and finish the job they started."

Tears came up in DeeDee's eyes. She winked them away.

"What are we going to do?" she asked. "We can't leave him out here to die."

Del drew in a deep breath.

"Maybe Danny can help him if we can get him

back to the house. Do you think we can carry him without hurting him too much?"

"If we're careful."

The boys took off their jackets and improvised a stretcher for the wounded fawn. Then, tenderly, they placed him on it. DeeDee walked beside him, her hand on the fawn's back in an effort to keep him from struggling while the boys carried the litter home. Soon after they left the woods and started across the clearing to the house, Danny saw them and came running.

"What's the trouble?" he asked.

"We found this little guy in the woods," Del said. "Somebody tried to kill him with an arrow."

"Let me take a look at him," Danny said.

The triplets stood by watching while he examined the wounded fawn.

"What do you think, Danny?" Fear tinged Del's voice when he was finally able to speak. "Is he going to be all right?"

Danny's lips narrowed.

"He's terribly feverish. It looks to me as though he could have carried this arrow for several days. He may have infection from it."

Del's gaze met his. "Is there something we can do?" he asked.

"Take him to the barn and make him a bed of straw. I'll call the vet and the game warden."

The triplets did as they were told.

"The poor little guy," Del muttered under his breath. "The poor little guy."

* * *

Carmen Roper stared up at her husband who was standing just inside the door. His hair was tousled and there was a wild, uncontrolled look in his eyes. At first thought she figured he must be drunk. Only liquor would twist a man's features so. Her entire being chilled.

She had known Clarence to take a drink once in a while if he was with some men who urged it on him, but in all the time they had been married she had never seen him when she even suspected that he was drunk. When he spoke, however, his voice was clear and firm. She knew that he was sober.

"Hello, Carmen," he said hesitantly, as though he didn't want to speak, but the words were forced past his thin lips.

"Hello, Clarence." In spite of her effort to remain calm, her voice tensed and shook slightly.

"Are–are the kids in bed?" he asked.

She nodded. "It's after ten, and they always go to bed at nine o'clock. They should be asleep by now."

"Good." He crossed the room to an easy chair and dropped into it wearily, as though the effort of walking had drained him of strength. "I came back about eight thirty but thought I'd hang around the barn until they were in bed and asleep before I came to the house."

Carmen watched her husband curiously. He had more to say. She could tell by the way he acted, but he only looked at her, breathing heavily. She waited, as someone waits for a blow to fall.

"Have–have you had anything to eat?" she asked him finally.

"I'm not hungry." The razor edge came back to his voice.

Carmen moistened her lips uneasily and waited. It was coming now. He was going to tell her that he was giving her a choice. She could turn her back on the Lord and forget that she had ever thought about following the Christ Rosalita and her family loved so much or she could get out of his life and stay out of it. Desperately she prayed for strength and courage.

At last he spoke. "I've got to talk to you!" he rasped.

Her cheeks whitened. "I–I'm sorry that you–you feel the way you do about my be-be-becoming a Christian, Clarence," she began, stumbling over the words in her consternation. "You know how much I love you."

It was as though he had not even heard her. Emotion twisted his face, and his eyes flashed.

"I went out of here this morning as mad as I've ever been at you in all the years we've been married," he told her. "It's the first time that I felt I thoroughly hated you."

She winced. "I know." For an instant she was afraid the anger was beginning to build again. "I've been terribly sorry I made you so angry," she went on, faltering. "I didn't want to."

Clarence frowned darkly. "When I took off, I was sure of what I was going to do," he went on, his voice rising. "I wasn't going to have you defy me. I was going to send you away the way I did the triplets."

She eyed him curiously. She wasn't sure yet just what he meant by what he was saying. It sounded as though he had given up the idea of making her leave. Yet, she could not be sure.

"I rode Joe harder today than I've ever ridden a horse in my life," he went on. "It's a wonder I didn't break his wind."

The lanky rancher leaned forward, his taut face inscrutable. It seemed that he had to get it all out, to tell her exactly what he had been considering and how he made up his mind.

"Finally I cooled off enough to begin to do some serious thinking," he said. "I thought about Rosalita and Jerry and their kids. You know, I used to give them a lot of trouble about that religion of theirs, Carmen. I rode them so much about it I wouldn't have blamed them if they'd never spoken to me again. But it didn't seem to make any difference how I treated them; they were always as nice to me as if I were the best friend they had."

Carmen said nothing. What Clarence said about

Rosalita and Jerry was certainly true. He had never lost an opportunity to ridicule or to make fun of them. Usually he picked the most embarrassing time possible. He would needle them in front of strangers or in front of those he knew were antagonistic to the gospel.

Carmen didn't give them money very often. They had never asked her for it and didn't even send her the letters they sent out to acquaint people with their needs. But there were times when she felt that she had to give them something to make up for the fact that Jerry had never earned very much. When that happened though, Clarence never missed a chance to lash out at them for the fact that they didn't have anything.

In fact, although Rosalita was her only sister, Carmen had never treated her or her husband very well herself. She could read Rosalita's face well enough to know that it bothered her to be sneered at and ridiculed. But that had made no difference in the way they treated Carmen in return. Both Rosalita and Jerry had done very well at living their faith in front of her and Clarence.

"Then," her husband continued, still having to force out the words one by one, "I got to thinking about Phil. There's been a big change in his life in the past few months, Carmen."

"Philip has never been a bad boy," she countered loyally.

"I didn't say he was bad. I'm as proud of him as you are." For the first time she noticed that he was working his big hands nervously. "Only he's been a lot better in the months since he's been a–a Christian." He paused significantly. "What I'm trying to say is that I don't think being a Christian has hurt him any."

Incredulously Carmen stared at the man who was her husband. *There must be something wrong,* she said inwardly. *Clarence must be talking about something else and someone else other than Philip. He can't possibly be agreeing that the gospel hasn't hurt Phil. He is too proud, too opinionated, himself, to make such an admission. Even if he felt that way, he wouldn't speak out, admitting that he had been wrong.*

Clarence wasn't finished yet, she realized. He was laying the groundwork for something he wanted to say. In a minute or two his anger would explode.

But she was mistaken. When he went on, his voice was hushed and charged with emotion. "I've spent the day riding around and thinking, Carmen," he said. "I suppose it's the first time in my life that I've spent a whole day just thinking things out."

He jerked upright. "I should've done it a long time ago. A man ought to get some of these things squared in his mind."

Carmen sat erect, her breath coming in quick, short stabs.

"You've been such a wonderful wife and mother that I've got no kick coming. If you want to go crazy over religion, I guess that's your privilege, as long as you don't try to shove it down my throat. I have no cause to blow my stack at you!"

It wasn't true! It couldn't be! The strength seemed to go from Carmen's knees, leaving her weak and trembling. God had answered her prayers! Clarence wasn't even going to argue with her or find fault. He was accepting her just as she was.

"Clarence!" she cried. "Do–do you mean that?"

"I must be out of my ever-lovin' mind talking to you like this." He stopped, and it was some time before he was able to continue. "But I've decided that I can't live without you, Carmen, as much as I object to this fanatical religion of yours."

He came forward and grasped her tiny hands in his.

"Will you forgive me?"

"Forgive you?"

Suddenly she was in his arms!

* * *

Carmen had never known what happiness was before that evening. She had made her choice for Christ, knowing as she did so that it might cost her her home and family. But God, in His mercy, had given Clarence back to her and their relationship was more tender and gentler than it had ever been before. She sang as she did her housework and turned the volume up to listen to the preacher who, by this time, meant a great deal to her.

Philip and Marie noticed the change that had come over their parents. They didn't say anything about it, but the same joy was reflected in their lives. Philip, especially, seemed to blossom as he gradually became aware of the fact that his dad was no longer objecting to his Bible reading and prayer.

Clarence, too, felt the happiness of the relaxed atmosphere. Once the tension was gone, he found that the family was happier and closer together than he had ever known they could be. He didn't say anything to Carmen about it. He had the sneaking feeling that if he did, she would start talking about thanking God or something like that, which might make him angry. But he was grateful, nevertheless. Life at the Circle R was more like it had been the first year they were married.

It was almost two weeks after Carmen confessed her decision to Clarence that he had to go to town for supplies. He wanted her to ride with him, but she had something else to do that day. He had run his errands and stopped in the filling station for gas before going home when he met an old rancher friend. They went into the cafe next door for a cup of coffee.

"Well, how're things out at the Circle R?" his neighbor asked.

"Okay." Clarence eyed his friend obliquely. There was something strange in Ed Harper's tone.

Ed grinned crookedly. "That's not the way I get it."

Clarence's eyes narrowed. "What do you mean by that?"

"I hear you've been havin' some trouble with Carmen lately."

Clarence's cheeks darkened slightly. "Quite the opposite," he countered. "Carmen and I have been happier than we've ever been."

"Come off it, Clarence," Harper exclaimed with the easy familiarity of one who has been a good friend for years. "I know better than that. A couple of your hands stopped by my place yesterday and said that wife of yours has gone nuts over religion."

The rancher sat up straight. "That's our business, isn't it?"

"Everybody in the valley's talkin' about it."

Harper didn't catch the warning signals in Clarence's tone. "They must not have much to talk about. That's all I can say."

"I told my woman if she ever got that way, I'd cut me a good club and beat it out of her." The corners of his mouth lifted. "Is that what you did?"

Clarence's eyes focused on him. "What Carmen does or doesn't do is none of your business, Ed," he retorted. "And it's nobody else's business either, except hers and mine."

"You don't need to get so huffy about it."

"I'm not gettin' huffy. I'm just telling you, so you'll get it straight. I don't understand this religion of hers.

I don't see what she can get out of sittin' around the house readin' the Bible and listenin' to sermons. But I can tell you this much. She used to be mighty hard to live with. There isn't a woman in the county who could've beat her when it came to naggin'. But that's all over with now. She makes the kids mind without screamin' at 'em, and she's singin' around the house instead of yellin' at me. So, you just keep still about that religion of Carmen's. Okay?"

# CHAPTER 9

# DEL'S CHARGE

The Davis triplets stayed out in the barn with the injured fawn until the game warden arrived an hour or so later. He got to the Orlis home in the country a few minutes ahead of the veterinarian. His eyes grew hard as he saw the arrow still sticking out of the little animal and the tuft of hair the triplets had picked up.

"Like I told you on the phone," Danny said, "there was a big blotch of blood out in the woods near the place where the kids found the fawn. Apparently, whoever shot this little guy also put an arrow into his mother."

The game warden examined the arrow as carefully as possible without touching it.

"We've always had a few poachers around here," he said. "They give us quite a lot of trouble. But this is the first time I've ever come across anybody who poached with a bow and arrow."

Doug spoke up quickly. "I sure hope you catch him. Anybody who would do a thing like that ought to have to spend enough time in jail, so he'll know better than to try it again."

"Oh, we'll catch him," the warden said confidently. "We always get the poachers sooner or later. They either get careless or we stumble onto a lead that gives them away. The thing that bothers me about this business, though, is knowing that the guy who did this will probably kill off a number of other deer before we're able to arrest him."

He turned to Danny. "You'd better take the kids into the house now, Mr. Orlis," he said. Something about his tone brought fear to Del's eyes.

"Why?" he demanded. "Why can't we stay out here? Why do we have to go in the house?"

It was obvious that the game warden didn't want to tell them. He glanced in their direction and then looked away quickly.

"I just think it's better," he hedged. "That's all."

Danny spoke softly. "Isn't there any other way?"

The warden shook his head.

"I wish there was. I don't like this sort of thing any better than you do. When a deer gets a wound as bad as this one has, the humane thing is to kill him. It would be cruel to let him live."

Del came flying back. "You can't do that!" he cried in desperation. "You can't kill him!"

The warden's eyes softened. "Believe me, son, this isn't any easier for me than it is for you. But I don't know what else to do. It's better to destroy him quickly than it is to let infection kill him an inch at a time."

"But I called the vet," Danny explained. "He should be here any time."

The game warden stared at Danny. It didn't seem logical that a man would send for a veterinarian just to save the life of a fawn.

"Do you mean to tell me that you called the vet for this deer?"

"I figured he would be able to remove the arrow and treat the infection from this wound," Danny told him.

The game warden straightened. "What do you plan on doing with the deer if you are able to pull him through?"

"If it's all right with you, we'd like to make a pet of him."

"I don't think you would be able to pen him, Mr. Orlis," he said. "Right now, he's gentle and all of that, but when he gets grown, he could be dangerous."

"I know that," Danny replied. "We wouldn't plan on penning him. We'd just like to keep him around the place, let him come and go as he pleases."

The officer thought about that. "Well, I can't see that that would hurt anything," he said. "And, as long as you've called the vet and are willing to pay him, the least I can do is to give him a chance to work on the fawn."

"Thank you," Danny said, smiling.

The triplets sighed their relief.

"I'll tell you what I'll do," the warden continued. "I'll stop back in a couple of days or so. If the infection is beginning to clear up and it looks as though the little guy has a chance of making it, we'll not destroy him. Otherwise, we'll have to go ahead with our original plan."

Danny nodded. "Fair enough."

The triplets thanked him profusely.

"You'd better save some of those thanks," he said gruffly. "I didn't say I wasn't going to kill the fawn. We still might have to do it."

"But–" Del protested.

"I just said that I was going to give the vet and you a chance to save his life first. I can tell you right now that I don't think you've got much of a chance. That infection has got a strong hold on him, and these little animals aren't always too strong to begin with, especially when they don't have a mother to take care of them."

Del was not dismayed. "He's going to be all right," he said, a new confidence in his voice. "I know that he's going to get well."

"I hope you're right," the officer told him. "I sincerely hope so."

With that he got into his car and drove away.

"What do you think, Danny?" DeeDee asked numbly. "Do you think we can keep him alive?"

The veterinarian from town arrived at the Orlis home half an hour after the game warden had driven away. He examined the little fawn tenderly and prepared to remove the arrow while the triplets watched.

"I'm not equipped to keep a fawn at our office," he said, looking at Danny, "so I brought my instruments out here. Want to help me?"

Danny started to agree, but checked himself.

"I could do that, Doc, but Del here has a way with animals, and he and his brother and sister found the fawn. Why don't you let him help you?"

The veterinarian frowned. "Think you can?" he asked the Davis boy.

"I believe so – if you'll tell me what to do."

His attitude seemed to satisfy the doctor.

"Okay. The first thing we'll have to have is a table to lay him on while we work."

By the time the vet was ready, Del and Doug had returned with an old kitchen table. They laid the fawn on it and the vet administered the anesthetic. Once the little animal was asleep, the doctor set to work methodically. Del handed him the instruments he needed and helped hold the fawn so he couldn't move while the vet was working. The entire operation only took a few minutes. He cut out the arrow, cleaned the wound as best he could, sterilized it, and sewed it up.

"I'll give him a shot of penicillin now and leave a couple of shots with you. You can give them tomorrow and the next day."

Uncertainty flecked Del's eyes. "I don't know whether I can do that or not," he said uneasily. "I never have."

"I'll help you," Danny said, taking the penicillin and syringe.

"You won't find it too difficult," the veterinarian said. "And if I'm out this way in a few days, I'll stop by to see how he's making it."

Del walked to the door with the intense young vet. "Do–do you think he's going to be all right?" he asked, speaking hesitantly.

The doctor pivoted slowly. "It isn't always easy to say. He's mighty sick right now. The infection had time to get a good start, and he's only a little guy to begin with. He hasn't too much to go on." He got into his car and put down the window so he could finish talking to Del. "We've done all that we can for him, Del, but frankly, I'm not too optimistic about his chances."

Del felt the muscles in his throat tighten, and the pain deep within him continued to grow. That was about what he had expected, but somehow, having to put it into words made it seem worse.

"Is–is there anything else we can do?"

The veterinarian paused. "His mother is dead, so he'll have to be fed by hand, and that's going to be quite a job."

"Oh, I don't care about that," the boy replied quickly. "Just tell me what to do, and I'll take care of him."

"First, you could try to get some warm milk down him and see that he's kept warm and dry. That's the only thing you or anyone else can do now. The penicillin will have to do the rest."

Del stood in the yard until the car was gone.

"Did he say what we can do now?" DeeDee wanted to know.

He nodded. "I've got to get a couple of baby bottles somewhere," he said, "and then we've got to feed him by hand to make sure he eats."

"I'll help you."

"So will I," Doug put in.

Danny said he would buy bottles that afternoon, but Del went over to the neighbors who had a new baby and borrowed them. With DeeDee's help he heated some milk and tried to get the fawn to eat.

It wasn't easy to get the fevered little animal to take the warm milk, but he worked with him patiently until he had emptied two bottles. The very effort of eating seemed to exhaust the fawn, and he soon went to sleep.

"There," the boy said under his breath. "That ought to make you feel better for a while."

DeeDee brought an old blanket and spread it

over the injured animal. "Now he won't get cold," she said quietly.

Del sat down on the hay beside the fawn.

"It's about time for dinner," Doug reminded him. "Hadn't we better go in?"

"You guys go ahead. I'm going to stay out here."

"He'll sleep for an hour or two."

But Del would not consent to leave. He stayed with the fawn all afternoon, except for the time it took to warm milk again and put it in the bottle. The fawn lay with his eyes closed most of the time. There didn't seem to be any change in his physical condition.

When Kay had dinner ready that evening, she turned to Doug who had come in from the barn a few minutes before.

"Would you please run out and tell Del that it's time to eat?"

DeeDee spoke up quickly. "He asked me to see if you'd fix him a sandwich and let me bring it out to him. He doesn't want to leave the deer in case he'd get the covers off or something."

Kay smiled. "I suppose that will be all right this time," she said, "but you can tell that young man for me that I'll not have him making a habit of it."

Del fed the fawn once more shortly after he finished the sandwich Kay had made for him. Getting his sleeping bag, he rolled it out on the hay near the injured animal.

"You won't need to be afraid tonight," he said, a

caress in his voice. "I'm going to be right here with you so I can take care of you."

He spent the night alone beside the injured animal. Although he crawled into the sleeping bag from time to time, he scarcely slept at all. Every time he closed his eyes, guilt and concern swept over him. Maybe there was something he should do for the fawn. Maybe the little animal would need him and he would be asleep. Something might even happen to the fawn that he could prevent if he remained awake.

He got up regularly to look at the fever-racked animal, talking to him in low, soothing tones. Once during the night he fed him another bottle of milk. That time the deer gulped the milk greedily.

Del's spirits soared. It seemed to him that the fawn was slightly better. At least he moved his head quicker and with more strength, and his fever-glazed eyes showed more expression.

Del scarcely dared to let himself think the fawn was making progress for fear it was just his imagination.

Del wasn't the only member of the family who was concerned about the fawn. All of the others had come out to the barn to see how he was doing. And, shortly after daylight, Danny was up and dressed and came out to check on Del and the little deer. The instant he stepped into the barn, his shoes crunching the dry hay, the boy was awake.

"Hi, Danny," he said, scrubbing at the sleep in his eyes with a knotted fist.

"How's our patient this morning?"

"I don't know for sure." He spoke hopefully, as though expecting Danny to confirm his hesitant appraisal. "But he seemed to me as though he was a little better."

Del crawled out of the sleeping bag and joined Danny as he knelt beside the fawn. Briefly Danny studied the injured animal.

"You know, Del, I believe he is better. He looks more alert to me."

Del brightened noticeably.

"That's what I thought during the night when I fed him, but I was almost afraid to say anything about it. I've been wanting him to get better so much that I was afraid maybe my imagination was playing tricks on me."

Danny put out his hand to pet the tiny deer, but the fawn wasn't having it. He jerked away, eyes rolling and his shoulder muscles trembling under his skin. For an instant he acted as though he was struggling to stand.

"Hey, there. What's the matter? I'm not going to hurt you."

"Take it easy, little guy." Gently Del extended his own hand. "Nobody's going to hurt you. Don't get so touchy."

Although the deer watched him intently, he gave no visible evidence of fear as Del stroked his neck.

The animal seemed to sense that Del was not going to hurt him.

"As long as I'm out here," Danny said, "I think we'd just as well give him his shot of penicillin for the day."

"I'll hold him for you, Danny," Del said.

Together they gave the fawn the injection of penicillin. He flinched as the needle stabbed into his skin and his eyes rolled, but Del talked to him soothingly and he relaxed almost immediately.

That afternoon the fawn definitely showed that he was better. When Del finished feeding him, he struggled to his feet and stood there, wobbly and trembling. Del chortled with glee.

"Look at him!" he exclaimed. "Just look at him! He's going to be running around the yard eating grass and hay in no time."

"Isn't it wonderful?" DeeDee asked. Her voice lowered. "You know, Del," she confided, "I prayed for him last night."

"So did I."

The next morning, they gave the fawn another injection of penicillin, and that afternoon he got up and stumbled awkwardly out into the yard, his toothpick legs stiff and clumsy.

"He's going to be all right," Doug said.

"You don't know how happy I am about that," Del replied.

"We all are."

# CHAPTER 10

# THE INVITATION

When the game warden came by the Orlis home several days later, the fawn was frisking about the yard as lively as though he had never been wounded. He watched the animal with amazement.

"If I didn't know it to be true," he said at last, "I'd say that deer couldn't possibly have been about to die with infection a few days ago."

Danny nodded. "He's certainly made good progress," he said. "A lot more than I ever thought possible."

After they talked for a few minutes, Danny asked for permission to keep the fawn.

"I don't see how I can deny you that. He wouldn't even be alive if you hadn't taken care of him the way you did."

Del's eyes widened. "Does that mean we get to keep him?"

The warden smiled. "That's right. You can keep

him here, although I wouldn't like to see him penned up, as I told you the other day. I don't think that's fair to the animal."

"We'll let him run. You don't have to worry about that."

The warden made a notation in the little book he carried.

"There is something I want to tell you," he said. "I must warn you again about him. A fawn is a cute little animal, and some people get the mistaken idea that they always stay that way. But that isn't necessarily true. Sometimes they do and sometimes they don't. This is especially true with males. An adult buck deer can be very dangerous."

"I was telling the kids the same thing last night," Danny said. "I've known a number of people who have been hurt by so-called tame deer. They forgot that deer are wild by nature and got careless around them."

"You won't have to worry about us with this little guy," Del put in. "We'll be careful. And besides, he's going to be so tame by the time he gets grown that he won't hurt anybody."

When the game warden was gone, Del once more turned his attention to the deer.

"Come on, boy. Come on." He held out his hand. "Come on over here and see me. I'm your friend. Or don't you remember?"

The fawn took a step or two in his direction,

uncertainly, remembering the kindness Del had shown him. But then his natural fear came rushing back and he jumped stiffly away. Del continued to talk to him, but for a moment or two did not try to get closer.

"I know what I'm going to call you," he said. "Your name's going to be Jumper because you jump around so much."

He took a step or two forward, cautiously.

"Come here, Jumper. Come here. You and I are friends. Okay?"

Del was able to approach the little deer by moving forward slowly and without making any sudden moves. Finally he was able to put his hand on the fawn's head. The deer wasn't entirely sure he liked it. His eyes rolled and his legs trembled with fear, but he remained comparatively still. The soft hand and equally soft voice were reassuring. They seemed to tell him that he had nothing to be afraid of, that he was not going to be hurt.

Del wanted to throw his arms about the fawn the way he would a big dog, but he knew from experience that such a move would terrify the already uneasy fawn. So he continued to talk to Jumper, stroking the soft hair on his neck.

In the house Doug watched what was going on from the kitchen window.

"DeeDee and I found that fawn too, Danny," he

complained. "I don't see why he belongs to Del all of a sudden. He acts as though he owns him."

DeeDee spoke up. "Neither do I. Actually, he should belong to me. I'm the one who found him first."

Danny went to the window and, putting his hand on Doug's shoulder, asked quietly, "Do you remember how it was during the basketball season?"

Doug eyed him.

"You were on the starting five and Del couldn't even play well enough to do more than get in the game for a couple of minutes when your team was about twenty points ahead."

"What does that have to do with this fawn?" Doug wanted to know.

"When I talked with Del then, I told him that God has given each of us different interests and talents. You're seeing his talent now. Look at the way he's able to handle that fawn."

The corners of the boy's mouth drooped. "I could do that too, Danny," he said, "if Del would only let me get close enough to him. But he won't. Every time I come near, Del has to stick in."

Danny shook his head. "I don't think any of the rest of us can approach that deer the way Del does. I thought I could, but I can't. I tried it."

DeeDee looked up at Danny plaintively. "But the fawn belongs to all of us," she protested. "We want him to love us too."

"Oh, he'll love you in time," he assured her. "He'll

love all of us because we'll be so good to him, he'll trust us as friends. But I don't think there's any doubt about who he's going to belong to. The deer has already decided that."

It was not easy for Doug and DeeDee to accept the fact that the fawn had chosen Del as the one person above all others that he trusted and loved. He would allow Doug or DeeDee to approach him on occasion, but never for more than a moment or two. Even then, he eyed them warily and went bounding away at the first unfamiliar noise or quick movement.

He would approach Del fearlessly, completely relaxed when he was beside him. He would press his head against the boy's leg, pleading with him to scratch behind his ears, or lean against his leg. He soon took to muzzling for a cube of sugar in Del's pocket. And when the boy walked away, Jumper would follow for a few steps as though he still wanted to be with him.

The fawn improved rapidly under Del's loving care. Soon he was running around as freely as though he had never been hit by a hunting arrow. He learned the sound of Del's voice and came running in response to it in that strange, stiff-legged gait of his.

"Look at him, Danny," Del said proudly. "Isn't he a beauty?"

Danny nodded. "I never get tired of watching a fawn. I don't think there's a more beautiful animal in this part of the country than a little deer."

"That's the way I feel. You know, Danny, I wouldn't trade him for that horse Uncle Clarence gave me to ride when we were in Texas last year."

Danny was grateful for that. He had been somewhat concerned that the kids would begin to miss the material things the Ropers had been able to give them. He was glad for a statement like this from one of them.

As time went on Jumper ranged farther and farther away from the Orlis home. Once he came down to the lakeshore while the boys were fishing and stood there, watching them curiously. Another time Danny saw him across the road half a mile or so away. The triplets, especially DeeDee, were disturbed about the fact that their new pet was getting farther and farther away from the house.

"If he doesn't stay closer, I'm afraid he's going to get killed by those game poachers, Danny," DeeDee said. "Isn't there something we can do to keep him closer to home?"

"I don't know what it would be. The only thing I can think of would be to put him behind a fence, and I don't think we would want to do that, would we?"

"Oh, no!" she replied quickly. "That would be terrible!"

Danny tried to ease her mind by talking with her. "I don't actually think poachers would kill a fawn if they knew what they were shooting at."

"They did once," she reminded him.

"That's true, but I think it's better to run the risk of him getting shot and be free than to put him in a fence."

Del's smile was infectious. "I'm going to keep working with Jumper until I get him so tame, he stays around the yard," Del said confidently. "I've got to see to it that nobody shoots the finest pet I've ever had."

"I wish you could teach him to like me as well as he does you," DeeDee put in.

Del studied her serious young face, a new warmth flooding over him. It was like Danny had said. God gave each person a different talent. One of his was having a way with animals. In that moment he wouldn't have traded talents with anyone else in the world.

That night Del and Doug walked down by the lakeshore in the growing darkness looking for their pet fawn, but they could not find him. They went up on the road in the direction of town until they passed the place where he had been seen earlier in the day and down along the lakeshore where he often went.

"It's no use." Doug's disappointment was keen. "If he was around here anywhere, we'd have surely seen him, as long as we've been out looking for him."

But Del was not ready to give up. "He's got to be here," he said doggedly. "He's just got to be."

His brother sighed. "I wouldn't mind staying out here all night if I thought it would do any good, but Del, it's so dark we couldn't see him now unless we stumbled over him and fell. We could get within six feet of him and not even know he was there."

Del had to admit the logic of what Doug said, but he still felt that he had to keep looking.

"We can't quit now. That little guy may have been shot by an arrow again or–" He stopped suddenly, not even daring to think what might have happened to the lovable little Jumper.

They were still discussing whether to quit for the night or keep on searching for him when Danny drove up and settled the matter.

"Find him?" he asked.

"Nope."

"But we're going to keep looking," Del added.

Danny paused. "Don't you think it's best to quit now and get a good night's rest? Then we can go out in the morning and look for him when we've got a chance of seeing him."

"But, Danny–"

"He might even come back on his own if we give him a little time."

Del saw the wisdom of Danny's suggestion and got into the car without further protest.

The following morning as soon as it was daylight, he got up and wakened Doug.

"Come on, let's go out and look for Jumper."

Doug sat up, wiping away the sleep from his eyes. "So early?"

"We've got to get out and see what happened to him."

"But we haven't even had breakfast," Doug protested sleepily.

"We can eat when we get back."

Although Danny had fostered the hope that Jumper might return during the night, he was nowhere to be found. The Davis boys went down to the lake once more, searching carefully on either side of the game trail they knew he used. They walked down the lake almost half a mile and angled back through the woods on still another path.

At last they went back to the house, had breakfast, and went out again to look for Jumper. Danny took them along the road in the car. They drove almost to town before turning around and going past the house just as far in the other direction.

"I still can't figure out what happened to him," Del said.

"I can," Doug said. "I think he got shot or caught by somebody who wanted him for a pet."

Danny disagreed. "There's another possibility that I think is more likely to be true. Jumper is a wild animal, and the instinct for freedom in such animals is strong."

"But we've been good to him, Danny," Del said. "We nursed him back to health and fed him with a bottle and everything. He would even come when I called him."

"I know all of that, Del, but still God has put a great longing for freedom in the hearts of His wild creatures. It might be that Jumper's love for the forest is so strong he couldn't stay with us anymore." Danny turned in at the drive. "And only time will tell whether I'm right or not."

Del remained in the car for a moment after the others got out. He hated to lose Jumper, that was true, but the main thing was that he wanted him safe and well. If he just knew that he was all right, he would feel a lot better about it.

For that reason, he still insisted on looking for Jumper, and Doug and DeeDee agreed to help continue the search.

"We've got to check out every place he could possibly be just to be sure he hasn't been shot or hurt or something."

The three of them spent the entire week searching for Jumper before they finally gave up. Even then Del didn't want to quit.

"But I suppose we have to," he said. "There isn't anywhere else to look."

"I think the wolves got him," Doug observed.

"Don't say that!" DeeDee's voice was indignant.

The triplets went about their farm chores regularly, but all the fun was gone. Too much of what they were doing reminded them of Jumper.

They were still mourning their loss when a letter came to Danny and Kay from their Aunt Carmen in Texas. Kay put it in the bedroom and waited for Danny to read it before letting the triplets know about it.

That evening Danny went over it carefully.

"It's wonderful that Carmen is a Christian now, isn't it?" he asked.

Kay was unsmiling.

"Yes, but I can't help letting it bother me."

"That's a strange thing to say. I would think you'd be thrilled about it."

"Oh, I am thrilled that she's a Christian," she said, "but you know the reason they let us have the triplets was because Clarence didn't want to have anything to do with the gospel."

Danny untied his shoes and kicked them off. "That's true." He tugged at the lobe of his ear. "You don't mean that you're afraid they'll try to get the kids back, do you?"

She nodded. "I've known of things like that to happen. You know how upset Carmen was at having to leave them with us."

"There's nothing they can do," Danny said. "They both signed away their rights to the triplets, and the adoption papers went through. It's all settled."

Kay smiled her relief. "Then I suppose it's all right to show this letter to the kids?"

* * *

The triplets were not as excited about going to Texas to visit the ranch for a time that summer as Danny and Kay had thought they would be. They took the news calmly.

"We want to go," Del said, "only–"

"Only what?"

"We ought to be here in case Jumper shows up."

"If that happens, we can take care of him for you," Kay said.

"I don't suppose it'll happen," Del said without enthusiasm.

* * *

As soon as Cedarton Bible Institute dismissed for summer vacation, Jim Morgan went on the road traveling with a school gospel team. They went to Chicago, into Ohio, and south to the hometowns of a number of CBI graduates who were now pastoring churches. It was the middle of June before he got back to Fairview.

Danny was gone with the plane, but Kay and the triplets were home. As soon as Jim got his bags in his room, Doug and Del asked him to go fishing with them.

"I'd like to," he said, "but I've got something else to do tonight."

"Like what?" Del asked.

"It so happens that I've got a date."

"There might not be another time. We're going down to Texas to stay at the Circle R for a month. If you don't go with us now, you'll be out of luck when it comes to finding the fish. We won't tell you anything."

Jim grinned. "I'll tell you what I'll do. If you guys'll get everything lined up right away, I'll go out for an hour with you."

"An hour?" Doug groaned.

"Come on," Del said. "That's better than nothing." They were on their way down to the water's edge when Del stopped suddenly.

"Doug!" he exclaimed in a hushed voice. "Look over there!"

Doug stared in the direction he was pointing.

"I don't see anything."

"A little more to the right. See? It's Jumper!"

Sure enough. There on the rim of the forest stood the fawn, now grown taller by half a foot and without his spots. While they stared at him, he whirled with a fling of his head and went bounding away.

"He's all right," Del said, his voice hushed. "Jumper's all right! Now I can go down to Texas and have a good time!"

* * *

Shortly after dinner that evening Jim borrowed the car and drove into town to see Connie McCloud.

Strange, he was so uneasy about it. He had heard from her regularly all winter and spring, but there had been something disturbing about her letters – something he couldn't quite understand. There were times when he felt that her letters were written by a complete stranger – someone he didn't know at all. It had caused him to pray for her in the past few weeks with a new sense of urgency.

However, Connie seemed glad to see him in spite of the difference in her letters.

"I've been so anxious for you to come home, Jim," she told him. "I've missed you so much."

They went out to the car together.

"I've been anxious to get back to Fairview to see you too."

"I wish you could have come home for Fritz's funeral," she went on after a time.

"So do I." He had wanted to come at the time, but didn't feel that he had the money. "Danny's been telling me about the tremendous things that have been happening since. I understand there've been a lot of kids saved because of his testimony."

She nodded. "Not only kids. Adults have found Christ as their Savior too. One of our neighbors was over to the house just last night to talk about spiritual things with Dad. He said he first became interested when Fritz talked with him about Christ."

Jim turned the wheel and pulled slowly away from the curb. "That brother of yours was a wonderful

Christian, Connie. I only hope I'll be able to do half as much as Fritz did for the Lord in the years I have to serve Him."

Connie leaned back in the seat and closed her eyes. She hadn't realized how much she thought of Jim or how much she had missed him until now that he was back. He wasn't especially handsome, and there certainly wasn't a lot of excitement involved in dating him, but he was a good, solid Christian kid. He was fun to be with and at the same time had the effect of drawing her closer to the Lord. She had never dated a boy who was more comfortable to be around or one she liked any better. She found herself reveling in his company.

Jim misread her silence. To him she seemed cold and unresponsive, as though there was something she was trying to tell him but didn't quite know how to go about it.

"How have things been going, Connie?" He voiced the question fearfully.

She pulled in a deep breath. "Not very good."

"Oh?"

"I've had a terrible time." She told Jim about going with Ted Larson, about Fritz's sudden death, and the way she had felt about it. She confessed her bitterness toward the Lord, her failure to attend church, and her hatred of Johnny Larson.

"Well, Connie," he said, selecting his words with care. "I can understand how you felt toward Johnny.

It would be hard to see a person and know that if he hadn't gotten drunk and driven a car, your own brother would still be alive."

The corners of her mouth twitched. "But, Jim, you don't know what hatred does to a person. It was awful!"

He drove slowly about town. "You sound as though it's all over with now."

"It is." There was genuine warmth in her voice. "I can thank God for it. I finally prayed for help to get over the way I felt toward Johnny and his whole family, and God took it away."

"That's wonderful, Connie."

"But there's something I still have to do. I have to apologize to several people and ask their forgiveness." Jim started to say something, but checked himself when Connie continued. "I've treated my parents awful – just awful – especially when they tried to get me to go to church. And I want to ask Ted Larson to forgive me for the way I've treated him, and Pastor Reeves and Winnie too."

Happiness surged up in Jim's heart. This was something he hadn't expected. That night he knelt beside his bed and for a long while praised God for the changes Christ had made in Connie's heart. She seemed even sweeter and more lovable than before.

# THE
# DANNY ORLIS
# SERIES

The Danny Orlis series, by Bernard Palmer, delivers a blend of adventure, mystery, and suspense through various settings—from the Canadian wilderness to Guatemalan jungles. Danny Orlis, an adept outdoorsman, skilled athlete, and committed Christian, employs his quick thinking, calm bravery, and biblical solutions to confront everyday problems and hair-raising dangers. Early stories focus on Danny navigating school life, sports, and outdoor challenges, while in later books, Danny and his wife Kay provide wisdom and guidance to youngsters facing lifelike situations and challenges. Having sold over two million copies, this series has made Palmer a renowned author in Christian youth literature. Palmer is also the author of the Felicia Cartright series and various other series for Christian youth.